HUG ME SO I'LL KNOW

JIMI CLEMONS

Rain Publishing

KNIGHTDALE, NORTH CAROLINA

Jimi Clemons/Rain Publishing, LLC
PO Box 702
Knightdale, NC 27545
www.rainpublishing.com

Publisher's Note: This is a work of fiction. Names, characters, places, and incidents are a product of the author's imagination. Locales and public names are sometimes used for atmospheric purposes. Any resemblance to actual people, living or dead, or to businesses, companies, events, institutions, or locales is completely coincidental.

Ordering Information:
Quantity sales. Special discounts are available on quantity purchases by corporations, associations, and others. For details, contact the "Special Sales Department" at the address above.

Hug Me So I'll Know/ Jimi Clemons. -- 1st ed.
ISBN 978-0-9908453-1-7

Library of Congress Control Number: 2015939001

DEDICATION

This book is dedicated to the most important person in my life, my wife Amy. Your patience, love, and never-ending support is why I am who I am. Thank you for celebrating us for all these years. Your spirit of life and laughter has gotten me through some very tough times. The only thing you've ever wanted is for us to be together, happy, and healthy. I'll never forget the day you looked at me and said, "I'll never love you as much as I love Jesus." I knew at that moment that I could never let you go. And thank you for loving our son Kassidy the way you do. He loves and adores you. We're on our way Amy. To you I want to give everything, because you ask for nothing. Thank you for being all that Jesus has called you to be for our family.

ACKNOWLEDGEMENTS

First I'd like to thank the Savior of the world Jesus Christ! The one that gave up His life for us all. The one that died on the cross, was buried, and rose from the grave three days later. Jesus you died so that we could live, and for that I thank you. Thank you for not leaving us where we were, and I praise you in advance for where you're taking us. To my wife Amy and our son Kassidy. You two bring so much joy to my life. Life is good, but God uses you guys to make it great. You are God's double portion that has been such a huge blessing in my life. I love you in ways that only God can explain. To my mother and sisters, we have always taken care of each other, and we always will. We've been through, and have survived so much; to God be the glory we're still here! I love you. To my uncle Jimmie, it has been an honor to carry your name. You're a great man. To the rest of my family, I love you. Aunt Edna, God's gotcha! To my best friends, Jeff Lee and Matt Joyce, thanks for always having my back. You've held me up and sharpened me just as Jesus instructed you to. To Pastor Ken Pugh, thanks for filling the gaps. Thank you for being who you are, and all you continue to be in my life. To Mimi and Papa, you guys are amazing grandparents! He loves you both so very much and so do we. To the Croniser family, we love you all. To Steve and Pat Lee, thank you for every meal, phone call, and minute you've given us, we love you. To Chrystal Joyce, thanks for your love and dedication. Sorry about the worn out carpet, it's Jesus' fault! To Amanda Dismukes, you're next in line! Your seeds have grown into something amazing! Keep sowing! Becky, thanks for taking such good care of our sweet boy. You're going to be a great mom. To Tim and Diane Joyce, you have been great mentors and we love you. To Mrs. Josephine Farrar, you've invested so much time and love into our lives and marriage. Your wisdom is God-sent and greatly appreciated. We love you more than you'll ever know. To Tyrone and Tina Bailey, you've always been there, and we'll always be there for you. To Steve Werner, what a blessing to have you in my life. You're a real friend, and I love you. Thanks to Will and Sue Nordmam, your love is still turning good people into great! Audra we love you! To Pastor Jensen, Pastor Aubrey, Pastor Kerry, and Pastor Daniel, thanks for loving and embracing our family. You're all awesome leaders. To Tony and Linda, God's timing has been our blessing when it comes to you two. We love ya! To Joey Tollefsen, thanks for your patience with me. The logo turned out amazing! And thanks to the entire Cary Church of God Family. Thank you Dot Culbreth for being a wonderful mother. You did it right.

Jesus, please remind Dr. Martin Luther King, Jr. that his labor was not in vain. I'm truly living what he dreamed.

ONE

(It's a very hot and sunny June day in Loudell, Tennessee, as the senior class of 2014 is about to graduate from Loudell Sr. High School. With tassels in hand the kids stand up, flip their tassels, and throw their caps in the air. They can now look forward to beginning the next chapter of their young lives. Later that night, the small town streets are roped off. The fireworks are flying and the whole town is celebrating the big day. Just outside of town about two miles, there's a small lake that's been a hideaway for three best friends since fourth grade. A black kid named Devin Cox, a white kid named Joey Allen, and a white girl named Jenna Woods. Devin has been accepted to Shaw University on a music scholarship. He has one of the most amazing voices you've ever heard. Both Joey and Jenna were accepted to North Carolina State. Jenna wants to be a veterinarian, and Joey wants to be a Software Engineer. Shaw University is only two miles from N.C. State, so with their schools being so close, they can still be together. As they sit around the lake drinking beer that someone illegally bought for them, Devin stands up to make a toast.)

DEVIN COX: A toast!
(Both Joey and Jenna stand.)

DEVIN COX: To Loudell High, and the good times we've had!
(They all tap their cans together and take a big swig.)

DEVIN COX: One more, one more! To the City of Raleigh, and
the chaos we're bringing to it!
(Again they tap cans and drink.)

JOEY ALLEN: I've got one! To two of the best friends any human being could ever ask for. To Devin, and Jenna! Best friends
forever!
(They turn up their cans and finish their beers. After they toss
the cans on to the small pile they've accumulated Jenna steps
forward to give Joey a hug. After she steps back, Devin steps
forward to hug Joey only to meet resistance. Joey puts his hand
on Devin's chest to stop him.)

JOEY ALLEN: Devin, how long have we been friends?

DEVIN COX: Since the fourth grade.

JOEY ALLEN: And how many times have you hugged me?

DEVIN COX: Never.

JOEY ALLEN: So what makes you think you're going to now?
I said it in fourth grade, and I'm saying it now, I am not hugging another man!

DEVIN COX: Joey, we just graduated from high school! It's a
special occasion!

JOEY ALLEN: I repeat, I am not going to hug another man. Special occasion or no special occasion!
(Joey steps away from Devin over to Jenna.)

JOEY ALLEN: Now if you looked like this!
(Joey wraps his arms around Jenna.)

JOEY ALLEN: I'd hug you all day.

DEVIN COX: Oh it's like that? Devin can't get a little love?
(Devin turns away pretending to be sad.)

DEVIN COX: Fine. I'll just walk around the lake and love myself.

JENNA WOODS: Poor baby, come here.
(Jenna walks over to Devin)

JENNA WOODS: I'll love on you.
(Jenna wraps her arms around Devin. As he looks over Jenna's shoulder at Joey, he smiles.)

JOEY ALLEN: Oh all right! I'll hug ya, Devin!
(Joey walks towards Devin with his arms wide open to give him a hug for the first time. Right before they hug, Joey ducks under Devin's arms.

JOEY ALLEN: Gotcha!
(Devin turns around and chases Joey. After only a few steps, Devin catches him and they start to wrestle around.)
JENNA WOODS: Boys, behave yourselves!

(After a long hot summer, a few trips to the beach, and some family vacations, August arrives. The time has come for Jenna, Joey, and Devin to get their first taste of independence as college students. After lugging Jenna's suitcases and bags down the driveway, Jenna's parents, Jeff and Betty Woods, look at each other and take a deep breath. The reality of Jenna leaving has struck its final blow.)

JENNA WOODS: Well, it looks like your dream has finally come true, mom and dad. You have me out of the house.

BETTY WOODS: Now you know better than that, Jenna! We've never said a thing about you being out of the house.

JENNA WOODS: I'm just kidding, mom.

JEFF WOODS: Jenna, do you have enough money? Do you have your cell phone?

JENNA WOODS: Dad, we've gone over this list five times already. Yes, I have my cell phone, and yes I have enough money.

JEFF WOODS: What about Jo Jo?

JENNA WOODS: I'm leaving him here.

JEFF WOODS: Maybe you should take him with you. I'll go in and get him.
(Jenna's dad runs inside to grab Jenna's teddy bear Jo Jo.)

JENNA WOODS: Mom, I would rather leave Jo Jo here, why do I have to take him with me?

BETTY WOODS: Jenna, it's not the bear. Your father's going into the house because he doesn't want you to see him crying. Pay attention to how long it takes him to get back, and when he does, look at his eyes.
(After being gone for almost ten minutes, Jenna's dad returns. As soon as he walks up to them, they can clearly see that he's been crying.)

JENNA WOODS: Don't be sad, daddy, I'm gonna be okay.

JEFF WOODS: I'm not sad, what are you talking about?

BETTY WOODS: Jeff, stop lying and tell your daughter that you're having a hard time with her leaving.
(As he nervously squeezes Jo Jo, Jeff looks down trying to hide his tears.)

JEFF WOODS: I just…
(Unable to fight it, he begins to cry. Jenna gives him a hug.)

JENNA WOODS: Dad, I promise I'll be okay. Please don't cry.
(Jenna gently touches her father's face.)

JENNA WOODS: Look at me, dad.
(With tears falling, Jeff looks into Jenna's eyes.)

JENNA WOODS: Everything you and mom taught me is right here, and right here.

(Jenna points at her head, and her heart.)

JENNA WOODS: You're the best parents in the world. You two are the very reason why I'm so excited about going to college, and making my dreams come true.
(Betty hugs Jenna as she begins to cry.)

BETTY WOODS: We're so proud of you, honey. You stayed away from drugs, you've never been in trouble with the law, and you've made honor roll all four years of high school. You've made us so proud, Jenna.

JEFF WOODS: Jenna.
(As Jenna wipes a tear from her left cheek, she looks up at her father.)

JEFF WOODS: Don't ever let anybody speak for you, and don't expect anybody to give you anything. You get out there, and earn what you want out of life. You hear me?

JENNA WOODS: I'll work hard, dad, I promise.

JEFF WOODS: Don't work hard, baby, work with wisdom. And make sure that your faith, is the foundation of your decisions, not your emotions.

JENNA WOODS: I understand, dad.
(Both Jeff and Betty hug Jenna at the same time. After a long loving embrace her parents step back.)

JEFF WOODS: You better get going.

JENNA WOODS: Yeah. Joey and Devin are gonna think I forgot about them.
(Jenna walks around to the driver's side and opens the door, as her dad puts her bags in the rear of her SUV. Just before she gets in, she hugs her parents one more time.)

JENNA WOODS: I love you guys.

JEFF WOODS: We love you too.
(Jenna gets in and starts the car.)

BETTY WOODS: Call us along the way to let us know you guys are all right.

JENNA WOODS: I will. I'll see you guys in about three weeks.
(Jenna shuts the door and clicks her seat belt.)

BETTY WOODS: We love you!

JENNA WOODS: I love you too!
(Jenna drives off waving and blowing the horn. As her parents watch her slowly disappear, they grab each other's hand.)

JEFF WOODS: Lord, please keep her under your blood.
(Across town, Devin and his mom Lucy are standing in the driveway waiting for Jenna. Devin looks at his watch.)

DEVIN COX: Where in the world is she?

LUCY COX: The good Lord said be anxious for nothing, Devin. I'm gonna assume that also means wanting to get away from your mother.

DEVIN COX: That's not what I meant, mama, and you know it.
(Devin puts his arm around his mom and gives her a kiss on the cheek.)

DEVIN COX: I want you to promise me that you'll take your medicine every day, and you'll get out and walk. The doctor said it would be good for you to get out at least four days a week and go for a walk. You have to exercise, mama.

LUCY COX: I know. I talked to Beatrice yesterday, and she said she would walk with me.

DEVIN COX: Good.
(Devin puts his hands on her shoulders.)

DEVIN COX: Mama, I hate leaving you here by yourself. I wish daddy were still alive.

LUCY COX: I do too son. Your daddy would be so proud of you. You're the first one in our family to ever go to college. Give me your word right now that you'll finish, and graduate from college, no matter what.

DEVIN COX: I will finish and graduate mama. With all the love I have in my heart for you, I promise.

LUCY COX: All I want is your word. Remember what your father told you about your word?

DEVIN COX: "A promise is what you make. But your word is who you are."

LUCY COX: That's right.

DEVIN COX: You have my word, mama, I will finish and graduate from college.

LUCY COX: I love you baby and I'm proud of you.
(Devin and his mom hug as she begins to cry. Off in the distance, they hear loud bass thumping music and a horn blowing. Jenna pulls into the driveway and gets out.)

JENNA WOODS: Hey, Mama Lucy!

LUCY COX: Girl, if you ever pull up in my yard with all that noise again, I'm gonna go get my hammer, and bust every speaker in that car! Do you understand me?

JENNA WOODS: Mama Lucy that's Fifty-Cent.

LUCY COX: I don't care if it's a dollar and thirty-five, don't you roll up in my yard with all of that hip hop noise again! Now come here and give Mama Lucy a hug!
(As she's holding Jenna, and Devin is putting his bags in the car, she whispers in her ear.)

LUCY COX: You've always been like a daughter to me, and I trust you. Please take care of my baby.

JENNA WOODS: I'll do my best, Mama Lucy.

DEVIN COX: What's all the whispering about?

JENNA WOODS: Don't worry about it, it's just girl talk.

DEVIN COX: Well, you two are gonna have to save it for later, because we need to get on the road.
(Devin gives his mom one last hug and gets in the car. Jenna winks at Lucy and mimes.)

JENNA WOODS: I'll take care of him.
(Lucy winks back.)

DEVIN COX: All right, mama, I'll call you when we get there!

LUCY COX: Okay. Be careful!

JENNA WOODS: We will!

DEVIN COX: Jenna, you want to see something funny?

JENNA WOODS: What?
(Devin cranks up the stereo full blast.)

DEVIN COX: Mama, didn't you tell her not to do that?
(Jenna yells out to Mama Lucy.)

JENNA WOODS: It wasn't me, it was Devin!
(Mama Lucy yells back.)

LUCY COX: You better be gone before I get back!
(Lucy heads for the house.)

DEVIN COX: Go! Go! Go!
(Jenna slams the gas pedal down and they take off. When Lucy reaches the door, she turns around and watches the car slowly disappear as she smiles and blows them a kiss. At last, they finally make it to Joey's. Walter Allen, Joey's dad, Judy Allen, Joey's mom, and Jessica Allen, Joey's ten-year-old sister, are all standing on the front porch when Jenna pulls in the driveway, they grab one bag each, and walk to the car.)

JOEY ALLEN: It's about time.
(Joey doesn't have a good relationship with his parents. He can't wait to get away from them. It's his sister that means the world to him. He wraps his arms around her and holds her tight wishing he could take her with him. Joey whispers in her ear.)

JOEY ALLEN: Make sure you do your homework, and stay out of their way. Don't give them any reason to yell at you when they start drinking. Just go to your room, and hang out there. I stashed snacks all over your room in case you need to stay in there for a while.

JESSICA ALLEN: I love you, Joey.

JOEY ALLEN: I love you, Jes.

(Joey sits in the back seat. Before he can even get in and get comfortable, his parents walk off without saying goodbye, leaving Jessica standing there.)

JOEY ALLEN: Remember what I said, Jes, stay clear.
(Jessica waves as Jenna pulls out of the driveway. Joey looks back at his parents hoping they might at least wave good bye. But all he gets is his dad yelling at his little sister.)

WALTER ALLEN: Jessica, get in this house now!
(Devin looks back at him from the front seat. He can tell that Joey's worried about Jessica.)

DEVIN COX: She's gonna be all right, man.

JOEY ALLEN: They better not hurt her.
(The three lifelong friends take a left out of Joey's subdivision, and hit the road headed for college in North Carolina. But college is not the only thing waiting for them. Those three old friends, tragedy, and death have set three appointments — appointments that come with absolutely no cancellations.)

TWO

(It's now mid-October, and the leaves have all changed, revealing yet another beautiful quality of the state of North Carolina. Devin has made lots of new friends on his campus, but he still spends most of his time with Joey and Jenna. After a long hard week of hitting the books, Friday finally arrives and it's time to let loose. While Devin waits for Joey to get out of the shower, he decides to get on the computer and check his e-mail. When Joey gets out of the shower, he puts his robe on and walks into the living room over to the mirror to brush his hair. His back is turned to Devin, but he can see him in the mirror sitting at the computer desk. While Devin is reading one of his e-mails, Joey says something that Devin never thought he'd hear him say.)

JOEY ALLEN: I'm in love with Jenna.
(Devin immediately spins the chair around to face Joey. After staring at him in utter shock for a few seconds, Devin responds.)

DEVIN COX: Please, tell me I misunderstood what you just said.

JOEY ALLEN: No, you didn't. I'm in love with her, Devin.
(Devin leans back in the chair and sighs.)

DEVIN COX: Joey, she's like our sister man.

JOEY ALLEN: Devin, that was all nice and cute when we were kids, running around telling everybody we were brother and sister. But it's different now, man.

DEVIN COX: I can't quite wrap my mind around this one Joey. Not to mention you have a girlfriend, and Jenna has a boyfriend.

JOEY COX: Scott doesn't care about Jenna. The only reason he's with her is because of a bet he made with some of his fraternity brothers. He knows she's never been intimate with a guy, and he bet them that she would be with him.
(Devin walks over to Joey and stands face to face.)

DEVIN COX: How do you know that?

JOEY ALLEN: One of his fraternity brothers was down at the Wolf's Den drunk, running his mouth. I was sitting at the table behind him. He obviously didn't know that Jenna and I are friends.
(Devin begins to slowly pace back and forth. Joey recognizes the look on Devin's face. He's only seen that look twice before, and each time it ended in Devin losing his temper.)

JOEY ALLEN: Will you give me a break with that pacing back and forth?

DEVIN COX: So you're telling me that this fool is using her to win a bet?

JOEY ALLEN: Yes.

DEVIN COX: Now you do know that there is no way I'm gonna sit back and let him do this to her. Where are they hanging out tonight?

JOEY ALLEN: She sent me a text earlier and said they were going to The Wolf's Den after the football game.

DEVIN COX: Is that the little bar on the corner across the street from Dominic's Pizza and Subs?

JOEY ALLEN: Yeah.

DEVIN COX: Well it's on. We'll roll up in there and deal with this fool.

JOEY ALLEN: Devin, don't go down there starting trouble. They've got two big bouncers working the door that wouldn't hesitate for one second to throw you across the parking lot.

DEVIN COX: I'm not going down there to start trouble. I just want to talk to him.

JOEY ALLEN: Why don't you talk to him when he's not drinking? You know how he is when he drinks.

DEVIN COX: All I want to do is talk to him. Now if he decides he wants to get froggy and jump, then it's just gonna have to go down like that!

JOEY ALLEN: Just be cool when you get there.

DEVIN COX: This is Devin you're talking to baby. Cool is all I know.
(After the big game, the football crowd begins to make their way out of the stadium. In spite of the thirty-five to zero romping the Tarheels put on the Wolfpack, everybody remains in party mode. Jenna, three of her friends, and her boyfriend Scott arrive at the Wolf's Den. When Devin looks up and sees them coming through the door, he leans over towards Joey.)

DEVIN COX: Look at this fool, man. It's not even seven o'clock and he's already drunk.
(When they get to the table, Scott stumbles over one of the chairs. Devin shakes his head in disgust.)

DEVIN COX: You need to sit down dude!

SCOTT GATTS: Devin my man! My brother from another mother!
(Scott plops down in the chair beside Devin, puts his arm around him, and gets right in his face.)

SCOTT GATTS: What's up, dawg?
(Jenna sits beside Scott and whispers to him.)

JENNA WOODS: Scott honey, why don't you sit back?

(Knowing Devin as well as she does, Jenna can see that Scott is treading on thin ice. But instead of taking Jenna's advice, Scott yanks his arm away from her.)

SCOTT GATTS: Whatever! I'm chillin with my man Devin.
(Devin leans to his right towards Joey to escape Scott's beer breath. After seeing the way Scott disrespected Jenna, both Joey and Devin are losing their cool.)

DEVIN COX: Okay, seriously, you need to chill, Scott!

JENNA WOODS: Scott, let's go out on the deck and get some fresh air.
(Again Scott yanks his arm away from Jenna.)

SCOTT GATTS: I don't want to go out on the deck! And stop grabbing my arm!
(Joey leans forward in his chair and begins to impatiently bounce his legs as he reaches his boiling point.)

JENNA WOODS: You're a jerk!
(Jenna grabs her purse.)

JENNA WOODS: Devin, Joey, I'll give you guys a call tomorrow.
(Scott grabs Jenna by her wrist and pulls her back towards him.)

SCOTT GATTS: Where do you think you're going?

JENNA WOODS: Let go of me, Scott!

DEVIN COX: Let her go, Scott!

SCOTT GATTS: I asked you a question, girl, where are you going?

JENNA WOODS: I said let go of me!
(Scott yanks Jenna by her arm causing her to stumble over one of the chairs.)

SCOTT GATTS: You're not going anywhere!
(Joey has had enough. He steps between Scott and Jenna.)

JOEY ALLEN: Come on, I'll take you home.
(Joey grabs Scott's wrist.)

JOEY ALLEN: Let her go, Scott!

SCOTT GATTS: Didn't you hear what I said, farm boy? She's not leaving!
(With all the patience he has, Joey restrains himself. Devin is keeping an eye on Scott's two fraternity brothers to make sure they don't make a move. Joey gets in Scott's face and yells.)

JOEY ALLEN: I said let her go!
(Joey reaches his breaking point and goes off the deep end. He grabs Scott by his throat, pushes him up against the wall, and begins to wail on his face one straight jab after another. As soon as Scott's two fraternity brothers stand up, Devin pushes one of them down, and punches the other one right square in the nose, knocking him flat on his back.)

JENNA WOODS: Joey, stop it! Stop!
(About that time, four bouncers steam roll their way through the crowd that's watching the fight. One bouncer grabs Devin, one bouncer grabs Joey, and the other two catch Scott as he slowly slides down the wall. After getting Devin and Joey outside, the bouncers ask them what happened. Jenna immediately speaks up.)

JENNA WOODS: This is my fault. These two guys are my best friends, and my boyfriend is the guy that was getting punched. My boyfriend is a little drunk, he got a little rough with me, and that's what caused all of this.

JOEY ALLEN: It's not your fault, Jenna. I know you guys don't want any fighting around here and I apologize for starting trouble. I threw the first punch, and that's what started the fight.

DEVIN COX: And I was just watching my boy's back.
(The bouncer turns to Devin.)

BOUNCER: I don't remember ever seeing you here before, what's your name?

DEVIN COX: Devin.
(Then he turns to Joey.)

BOUNCER: I've seen you here plenty of times. What's your name?

JOEY ALLEN: Joey.

BOUNCER: Look guys, I understand why you did what you did, that guy is an idiot. Every time I see him in here he's drunk running his mouth. If it were up to me, I would ban him from this place for good. But unfortunately, there are no rules here against being an idiot. But there are rules against fighting, and I'm gonna have to ask you to leave the premises. Just give it a week or so, and then come on back. Cool?

JOEY ALLEN: Sorry again for the trouble.

DEVIN COX: Sorry, man.

BOUNCER: Don't worry about it.
(Both Joey and Devin shake hands with the bouncer.)

BOUNCER: Every girl in the world needs friends like these. You're lucky.

JENNA WOODS: I know. That's why I love them so much.
(Just because their night at the bar has ended, doesn't mean their night on the town has. After leaving the bar, they go to a party at an apartment complex that a friend of Joey is throwing. Once they arrive, Devin, Jenna, and Joey decide to hang out in the parking lot before going in. Jenna opens the hatch of her SUV, and both she and Devin sit down, while Joey takes a seat on the curb. Joey is looking down at the ground rocking back and forth as Jenna and Devin laugh and talk. Devin leans over to Jenna and whispers.)

DEVIN COX: Look.

(Jenna looks at Joey and can clearly see that something is bothering him. She thinks it's the whole Scott incident that happened at the bar.)

JENNA WOODS: Joey, don't let Scott's drunken stupidity bother you. He's not worth it.

JOEY ALLEN: It's not Scott that bothers me, Jenna, It's you.

JENNA WOODS: Excuse me? What do you mean I bother you?

JOEY ALLEN: The fact that you would even get involved with a guy like that bothers me. I pegged you to be smarter than that.

JENNA WOODS: So what are you my father now?

JOEY ALLEN: Jenna, you can sit there and make light of it if you want to, but you need to check yourself. If you choose to date guys that are gonna smack you around and disrespect you like that, you really need to check yourself.

DEVIN COX: Has he ever been physical with you before tonight?
(The question makes Jenna a little uncomfortable. She stands up, and starts to slightly rock side to side as she talks to them.)

JENNA WOODS: Guys, give me a break!

DEVIN COX: J Weezy-

(Jenna looks directly at Devin after he calls her by the nickname he gave her their junior year of high school.)

DEVIN COX: Has he?

JENNA WOODS: He's pushed me a few times, but nothing serious.

JOEY ALLEN: You don't think pushing you around is serious? How do you think the beatings start? They start with a push here, a grab there, and then the next thing you know you're walking around with a black eye and busted lips.

JENNA WOODS: Will you please just get off of my back! Not everybody is like your father, Joey!
(Bringing up the physical abuse that Joey has witnessed most of his life upsets him. He stands up walks away.)

DEVIN COX: Now you know you're wrong for going there. Why did you say that, Jenna?
(Jenna takes a deep breath.)

JENNA WOODS: Joey, wait!
(Jenna goes after Joey leaving Devin by himself.)

DEVIN COX: Hey, Bonnie and Clyde, when you finish ripping each other's guts out, meet me up stairs! I'll be the one holding the long tube with the funnel on the end!
(Devin closes the hatch and joins the party upstairs. After catching up with Joey, Jenna grabs his shoulder and turns him around to face her.)

JENNA WOODS: I'm sorry for what I said. I was wrong, and so were you. Who I decide to go out with is none of your business, Joey. It's my life.

JOEY ALLEN: I wasn't trying to tell you how to live your life, I just want you to be okay. You had beatings coming Jenna, I could see it in him. It's very familiar to me. When he's sober, he's the sweetest thing in the world. And it's that same sweetness that tricks you into thinking that one day he's going to change. Over time, you convince yourself to hang in there, with all hopes of changing him. You cannot help someone that does not want to help themselves, Jenna. If we all could fix what's wrong with people, there would no problems in the world. Scott reminded me so much of my father tonight. The way he treated you, my dad acts the same way when he drinks. Then the next morning, he wakes up, and acts as if nothing happened. And my mom just goes right along with it. To me, that's just like telling him what he did the night before is okay. A man should never, ever put his hands on a woman if his intentions are to hurt her, no matter what she does. I've had to hold my sister, and rock her to sleep many nights because of my dad's abuse. And just like Scott, alcohol is always the trigger that fired the gun.
(Joey gently touches Jenna's right cheek.)

JOEY ALLEN: I would never, ever, do anything to hurt you. Do you know that?

JENNA WOODS: Yes.

JOEY ALLEN: Never.
(Joey steps forward and kisses Jenna for the very first time. Completely caught off guard, and shocked by his kiss, Jenna takes a step back.)

JENNA WOODS: What are you doing, Joey?

JOEY ALLEN: I just kissed the girl I'm in love with.

JENNA WOODS: Joey, this is a little too much for me right now. And to be honest with you, I'm a little uncomfortable. So let's stay away from the touching and kissing, so I can process all of this.
(Joey takes an extra step back and gives Jenna her space.)

JOEY ALLEN: I don't ever want you to feel uncomfortable because of me.

JENNA WOODS: It's not you that makes me uncomfortable, Joey, it's what you said. We've known each other practically all of our lives. And you've never said, or done anything that would let me know you feel this way. Where is all of this coming from? And why haven't you said anything before now?

JOEY ALLEN: I never said anything because I was afraid of losing my friend. I've seen friendships turn into relationships, and in the end, when it's all said and done, there's nothing left. And I didn't want that to happen to us. I don't want to lose your friendship. Nothing is worth that.

JENNA WOODS: I just, I don't know what to say. I'm shocked.

JOEY ALLEN: You don't have to say anything, just listen.
(Joey grabs Jenna's hand and walks over to a brick wall that runs alongside of the apartments.)

JOEY ALLEN: Have a seat.
(Jenna takes a seat, and a deep breath.)

JOEY ALLEN: Jenna, I don't want you to get all freaked out, and start treating me different. You're still my homegirl no matter what. And if friendship is all you're willing to give me, then so be it. As long as I have some part of you, I'm happy. But if you will, just think about trusting me with the other side of your heart, that doesn't say friend, I promise you on my life, that I'll take good care of it.

JENNA WOODS: What about Marie? You do remember that you have a girlfriend don't you?

JOEY ALLEN: I broke up with her.

JENNA WOODS: Did you break up with her because of me?

JOEY ALLEN: No.
(Joey grabs her hand, and pulls her up. After they're standing face to face, he answers her question.)

JOEY ALLEN: I didn't break up with her because of you. I broke up with her because she wasn't you.
(Again, Jenna is speechless.)

JENNA WOODS: You never cease to amaze me. Let's talk, take our time, and see where it goes. This doesn't mean we're dating, we're just seeing where things go.

JOEY ALLEN: That works for me.

JENNA WOODS: But if at any time at all, things get too weird, or our friendship is in jeopardy, we walk away. And, we walk away, peacefully as friends.

JOEY ALLEN: You have my word.
(Jenna steps forward and wraps her arm around Joey. As they hug, she smiles and whispers to him.)

JENNA WOODS: I can't believe this is happening.
(On October 29th, 2014 in Raleigh, NC, Joey Allen and Jenna Woods hold each other, with their hearts wide open to the possibility of love. But little do they know life is going to take them beyond what their love can withstand. They just don't realize that they're experiencing the beginning of their end.)

THREE

(Three years have gone by, and they're now beginning their senior year. They've survived the late night studying, the parties, and all the drama that comes with college life. Joey and Jenna are together, and very much in love. Devin, who is now known all over North Carolina for his soulful voice, has become somewhat of a celebrity. He's performed the national anthem at professional hockey games, all kinds of ACC sporting events, and even sang at the Governor's inauguration. But along with the popularity, also came the problems. And like some problems, you never realize you have them, until it's too late. Everywhere he goes, women are flirting, and giving him some very dangerous attention. People sometimes recognize him out in public, and ask for his autograph. Not only did Devin have the voice everybody wanted to hear, he also had the personality some began to hate. The accolades, the applause, and the new company he was starting to keep, was blindly taking him down. On their very first night back at school from summer break, Devin, Joey, and Jenna are hanging out at Devin and Joey's apartment.)

DEVIN COX: Can you believe we're seniors? In June, we're going to graduate, and be done with school.

(Devin holds his glass up for a toast.)

DEVIN COX: To no more school!
(Joey raises his glass. Jenna doesn't get in on the toast as she sadly looks at the two of them.)

JOEY ALLEN: Baby, what's wrong?

JENNA WOODS: After we graduate what's gonna happen to us? I don't want to graduate and hardly ever see you guys anymore.

DEVIN COX: I don't think that's going to be an issue for you two, Mr. & Mrs. Joey Allen.

JOEY ALLEN: Easy now.

JENNA WOODS: Devin, you're the one we should be concerned about. I can see you now, all over the T.V. singing and traveling the world. You're gonna forget all about us.

DEVIN COX: Ya got that right.
(Jenna punches Devin in the arm.)

JENNA WOODS: That's not funny.

DEVIN COX: I'm just joking! If I ever become famous, you better believe all three of us become famous. We're lifers.
(Again Devin raises his glass.)

DEVIN COX: A toast.

(This time Jenna gets in on the toast.)

DEVIN COX: To the future, and the friendship. May the two of them forever walk hand in hand!
(They tap their glasses together and drink. As Jenna grabs the bottle for a refill, the phone rings.)

JOEY ALLEN: I'll get it.
(Joey reaches back behind him to grab the phone off of the counter.)

JOEY ALLEN: Hello. Yeah hold on.
(Joey passes the phone to Devin.)

JOEY ALLEN: It's for you.

DEVIN COX: Hello. What's up Lorenz?
(Lorenz is calling to tell Devin about a party he's having.)

DEVIN COX: All right, cool.
(Devin hangs up the phone.)

JENNA WOODS: Who's Lorenz?

DEVIN COX: This guy I met on campus about a month ago. He's having a party tonight and he invited us.

JOEY ALLEN: Where does he live?

DEVIN COX: Clarkston Estates.

JENNA WOODS: Clarkston Estates! Home of the deep pocket parents and their spoiled rich kids.

JOEY ALLEN: What do his parents do for a living?

DEVIN COX: I don't know, and I don't care. Let's take a shot and roll out.
(They quickly slam their shots, call a cab, and head for the party. As they pull up they see cars lined up all the way down the street.)

DEVIN COX: Look at all of these cars.
(As the cab stops to let them out, the three of them can't believe the size of the house.)

JENNA WOODS: Is that his house right there?

DEVIN COX: 604 Fredricks Lane, that's it.

JENNA WOODS: Can you believe the size of these houses?
(As they walk up in the yard, almost immediately people begin to recognize Devin. Lorenz walks up to Devin and puts his arm around him.)

LORENZ BURT: My boy! You made it!

DEVIN COX: Man, your parents must be stacking mad cake. This house is huge.

LORENZ BURT: Forget the house. Come with me, I want you to see something.

(Before they turn and walk towards the house, Devin introduces his friends. First Joey, and then Jenna.)

LORENZ BURT: What's up, Joey!
(Lorenz shakes his hand.)

JOEY ALLEN: What's goin on, man?
(Lorenz then turns to Jenna.)

LORENZ BURT: Devin, you were right. She is gorgeous.
(Jenna and Lorenz shake hands as she modestly smiles.)

LORENZ BURT: It's nice to meet you.

JENNA WOODS: Nice to meet you too.

LORENZ BURT: So are you guys ready to throw down or what?

JOEY ALLEN: I thought you'd never ask.

LORENZ BURT: Come on in.
(As they enter the front door, Devin, Joey, and Jenna, are in
awe over just how beautiful the house is. After making their
way through the crowd, they walk into the den where they
find people sitting around talking, playing drinking games,
playing pool, and guitar hero.)

LORENZ BURT: Hey, Donnie, take good care of these two! Give
them anything they want.

(Donnie is the bartender running the full size, fully stocked bar Lorenz has in his den. Lorenz leans towards Jenna and Joey so they can hear him over the music.)

LORENZ BURT: You guys can head over to the bar. Donnie will take care of you, drink all you want. If you get hungry, there's plenty to eat in the dining room. I'm gonna steal this guy from you for a few minutes.
(Devin and Lorenz head up stairs.)

DEVIN COX: Where are we going?

LORENZ BURT: To your own little paradise.
(After climbing the long beautiful spiral staircases, they walk out on the upstairs deck. On the other side of the deck, is another small flight of stairs. When they get to the top of those stairs, Lorenz stops.)

LORENZ BURT: Now are you sure you're ready for what's behind that door?

DEVIN COX: It depends on what it is?

LORENZ BURT: I told you, your own little paradise.
(Devin looks at Lorenz with somewhat of a nervous look.)

DEVIN COX: What's on the other side of that door Lorenz?
(Lorenz opens the door, and Devin can't believe his eyes.)

LORENZ BURT: Welcome to paradise, my friend.

(In that room, away from the rest of the party, sitting at a table sipping on martinis, are three of the most beautiful women Devin has ever seen. One is Latino, one is black, and one is white. Devin can't believe his eyes.)

LORENZ BURT: You gonna go in or what?

DEVIN COX: What's going on here Lorenz?

LORENZ BURT: They're all for you. You can have one, or you can have all three.
(Devin looks at Lorenz.)

DEVIN COX: Are you kidding me?

LORENZ BURT: Go on in and have you some fun, man. The bar over there is fully stocked.
(Devin looks at Lorenz again.)

LORENZ BURT: Go ahead.
(With hesitation, Devin walks through the door.)

LORENZ BURT: By the way…
(Devin turns to face Lorenz.)

LORENZ BURT: This is not my parent's house. This is my house.
(Lorenz closes the door, leaving Devin in what he thinks is paradise, and what Lorenz has set for bait.

FOUR

(The next morning, after only three hours of sleep, Devin wakes up. To his left, he sees two of the girls. And to his right, he sees the other girl. He sits up, and squirms his way out of bed hoping he doesn't wake any of them. When he opens the door, the sun and his hangover clash, causing him to quickly close the door. He rubs his eyes, uses his hand for a sun visor, and walks out. When he gets down stairs, he sees Lorenz sitting at the dining room table eating breakfast. As Devin slowly crosses the room, Lorenz hears his feet dragging the floor.)

LORENZ BURT: There he is!
(Lorenz stands up and begins to clap.)

LORENZ BURT: How was your meeting with the United Nations?
(Devin can only shake his head.)

DEVIN COX: Lorenz, that by far, is the craziest thing I have ever seen. Who are those girls? And how do you know them?

LORENZ BURT: You can keep them if you want them? Or I could just get you a whole new set.

DEVIN COX: All right dawg, you gotta tell me what's up man. You've got this phat crib, you've got a ninety thousand-dollar Benz in the garage, and you've got fine women just lying around. How are you doing it, man? You're a college student. (Lorenz smiles at Devin.)

LORENZ BURT: Why don't you roll out with me for a little while today? I want to show you something.

DEVIN COX: The last time you said that, I ended up with the United Nations. What's next?

LORENZ BURT: You asked me how I'm able to have all of this, and I'm gonna show you. Just go on upstairs, take a shower, and let's roll out.

DEVIN COX: I need to go home first. I'm not gonna take a shower and wear the same clothes.

LORENZ BURT: You don't need to go home, grab something out of my closet. We're about the same size. And if you look in the very back of the closet, you'll find fifteen or twenty unopened packs of silk boxers, take as many as you want.
(Devin gets cleaned up, and both he and Lorenz hop in the Lexus, Lorenz's other car. After driving for ten minutes or so, Lorenz pulls into the parking lot of an office building.)

LORENZ BURT: What do you think about that building?

(Devin rolls his window down, sticks his head out, and looks up at the building. The building is about six stories tall with black stained glass windows.)

DEVIN COX: Well, I would say it's just a building. But knowing you, there's gotta be more to it.

LORENZ BURT: I own it.
(Devin quickly turns and looks at Lorenz.)

DEVIN COX: Yeah right.

LORENZ BURT: I'm serious. I own that one and two more just as big.

DEVIN COX: What are you into, Lorenz?

LORENZ BURT: This.
(Lorenz opens his glove compartment and pulls out a ten thousand-dollar money roll.)

LORENZ BURT: This is what I'm into. Having more money than I know what to do with.
(Devin can't believe his eyes.)

DEVIN COX: How much money is that?

LORENZ BURT: Ten G's. Pocket change.

DEVIN COX: Where did you get it?

LORENZ BURT: It doesn't matter where I got it. The question is, do you want to get it?
(Lorenz hands the money to Devin.)

DEVIN COX: Oh my goodness.

LORENZ BURT: It feels good doesn't it?

DEVIN COX: I cannot believe I'm holding ten thousand dollars.

LORENZ BURT: Bubble gum money, that's all that is. Child's play.
(Devin takes a deep breath.)

DEVIN COX: If this is child's play, I've got to get in the game. I'm down with this.
(Lorenz smiles as he sits back in his seat.)

LORENZ BURT: Meet me at that little convenience store down the street from fraternity row at 9:00 tonight.

DEVIN COX: Fraternity row? What's on fraternity row?

LORENZ BURT: You want to get in the game, that's where you start.
(Devin looks at the money, and then looks at Lorenz.)

DEVIN COX: I'll be there.

LORENZ BURT: I know you will.

(In Devin's eyes, meeting Lorenz is the beginning of new success. But in reality's eyes, meeting Lorenz will end as one of the darkest days of Devin's entire life. It's now 8:50 p.m. Saturday night, and Devin is on his way to meet Lorenz. He just can't imagine what he's in for as his curiosity builds. At 9:00 o'clock, Devin arrives to find Lorenz waiting on a narrow gravel driveway behind the little old convenience store. He parks his car and gets in the car with Lorenz.)

LORENZ BURT: You're on time, I like that.

DEVIN COX: Let's play the game.

LORENZ BURT: Let's roll.
(Devin and Lorenz take off for Fraternity Row. Fraternity Row is one long street of nothing but fraternities and sororities. As soon as Lorenz takes a left on Lee Drive, they begin to hear loud music.)

LORENZ BURT: Boy, they are wide open around here tonight.

DEVIN COX: Look at all of these drunk fools.
(Lorenz slows down to about three miles an hour, because there are people walking everywhere.)

LORENZ BURT: I love it.
(Lorenz parks across the street from the biggest party on Fraternity Row.)

DEVIN COX: Now what?
(Lorenz turns to Devin.)

LORENZ BURT: You wanted the playground, here it is.
(Devin looks around.)

DEVIN COX: I don't get it.

LORENZ BURT: You see that white car in the parking lot next to that sorority house?
(Devin looks to his left in the direction Lorenz is pointing in.)

DEVIN COX: Yeah.

LORENZ BURT: Watch this.
(Lorenz quickly flashes his headlights once. About one minute later, a young black guy gets out and joins the big party.)

LORENZ BURT: Now look over there.
(Lorenz flashes his lights twice, and a young white guy gets out of a car and joins the same party.)

DEVIN COX: Who are they?

LORENZ BURT: They work for me.

DEVIN COX: Doing what?

LORENZ BURT: They're part of my sales team.

DEVIN COX: And what do they sell?

LORENZ BURT: This.

(Lorenz pulls a black leather bag out from under his seat. In that bag, are a couple of smaller zip-locked bags of cocaine, along with several kinds of prescription drugs, and a bag full of ecstasy pills.)

DEVIN COX: You slinging dope Lorenz?

LORENZE BURT: No I am not. That's why I have those two that just went into the party. Other than what you see here in my hand, I've never touched the stuff a day of my life. That's the difference between a drug dealer and a smart businessman. A smart businessman will always keep his face hidden and his hands clean. Those two guys that work for me, have no idea what I look like. Look at where I'm parked, it's pitch dark. They don't even know the color of this car. All they've ever seen, are my headlights.

DEVIN COX: You call using two kids to sell drugs for you smart?

LORENZ BURT: They're not kids, they're grown men.

DEVIN COX: Lorenz, they couldn't have been any older than eighteen or nineteen.
(Lorenz pulls the passenger side sun visor down causing a small bright light to come on. He then opens his glove compartment, and pulls out a pocket size dictionary.)

LORENZ BURT: Look up the word adaptation.

DEVIN COX: For what?

LORENZ BURT: Just look it up and read it for me.
(Devin finds the definition.)

DEVIN COX: Adaptation. Got it.

LORENZ BURT: Read it.

DEVIN COX: A slow, unconscious modification of individual or collective behavior in adjusting to cultural surroundings.

LORENZ BURT: One is 30, and one is thirty-two. They look like college students, they dress like college students, they talk like college students, and through adaptation they become college students. That's the first lesson congress ever taught me. How to become a beneficiary of adaptation.

DEVIN COX: Congress?

LORENZ BURT: That's who I work for.

DEVIN COX: You're obviously not talking about the real United States Congress. So what are you talking about?

LORENZ BURT: A smart businessman also knows what not to say. But I tell you what, if you would like to find out yourself who congress is, I can make that happen.

DEVIN COX: I'm not trying to hook up with some drug lord, man.

LORENZ BURT: Be careful about what comes out of your mouth, Devin. I never said anything about any drug lord.

DEVIN COX: Let me see that.
(Lorenz hands him the drugs.)

DEVIN COX: Man, I promised my mother and father I would never allow drugs to be a part of my life. I can't do this, Lorenz.
(Lorenz sits there for a few seconds in silence.)

LORENZ BURT: You sure?

DEVIN COX: I can't do it.

LORENZ BURT: That's cool. I can respect that.
(Devin hands the drugs back to Lorenz. Lorenz puts them back under the seat.)

LORENZ BURT: If you change your mind hit me up, you've got my number.
(Lorenz drives off and heads back to Devin's car. Just before Devin gets out, he shakes Lorenz's hand.)

DEVIN COX: Good looking out, man I really appreciate it. It's just not my thang.

LORENZ BURT: It's all good.

DEVIN COX: I'll see you on campus.

LORENZ BURT: All right.
(Just after the door closes, Lorenz rolls the window down and calls Devin. Devin turns around, comes back to the car.

DEVIN COX: What's up?
(Lorenz peels off a hand full of hundreds from his money roll.)

LORENZ BURT: Take this.
(Lorenz extends the money to Devin and Devin pushes his hand back.)

DEVIN COX: Oh no. You can keep that.

LORENZ BURT: What's the problem?

DEVIN COX: The problem is that I can't afford to pay this money back. I'm sure there are some strings attached.

LORENZ BURT: It's not a loan, Devin, it's a gift.
(Devin stares at the money as he contemplates taking it.)

DEVIN COX: People don't just give people a stack of hundreds and not expect something in return.
(Lorenz grabs Devin's hand, pulls it towards him, and puts the money in Devin's hand.)

LORENZ BURT: Take the money, go out tonight, and have yourself a good time.
(After unlocking his eyes off of the money, Devin looks at Lorenz. As they both stare at each other, Devin can only think about what his mother has said to him a thousand times. She's

always said, "The devil's tricks will always look casual, before they become catastrophic." That was her way of telling Devin that deception can camouflage itself to claims its victim. But even with that warning ingrained into his heart, Devin allows the spirit of selfishness and greed to override wisdom, which unfortunately for Devin, will eventually end in sorrow and extreme grief.)

DEVIN COX: You sure it's not a loan?

LORENZ BURT: It's not a loan man.
(Lorenz pulls out a pen and a piece of paper.)

LORENZ BURT: Do you want me to put it in writing?
(Devin laughs and then takes the money.)

LORENZ BURT: You gotta learn how to relax, man. You're too young to be that serious.

DEVIN COX: Look at all of this money.
(He's so caught up in the stack of money in his hand, that he doesn't even hear Lorenz. And that's all Lorenz needed to see. He figures out that money is the best trap to set if he wants to catch Devin.)

LORENZ BURT: Did you hear what I said?

DEVIN COX: My fault, what did you say?

LORENZ BURT: Never mind. Look, I want you to really think about everything we talked about tonight, Devin. Now is your time man. The top of the world is waiting for you.

DEVIN COX: I'll think about it.
(After shaking hands and going their separate ways, the spirit of deception begins to do some of its finest work on Devin's mind.)

FIVE

(After a week or so of constantly thinking about the opportunity he has, Devin decides to call Lorenz. With Lorenz having caller ID, he sees Devin's name pop up on his cell phone. Lorenz smiles and says to himself.)

LORENZ BURT: Checkmate.
(Lorenz then answers the phone.)

LORENZ BURT: My man Devin.

DEVIN COX: What's up, Lorenz?

LORENZ BURT: You tell me.

DEVIN COX: I think it's time we take a trip to Capitol Hill.

LORENZ BURT: So you want congress?

DEVIN COX: I want money.

LORENZ BURT: All right. Meet me at my house Thursday night at seven. Cool?

DEVIN COX: Cool.

LORENZ BURT: Devin, if this goes as well as I think it's going to, a year from now, you won't even recognize your life.

DEVIN COX: Let's do it, man.

LORENZ BURT: I'll see you on Thursday.
(The time is set, the deal is done, and Thursday arrives. Devin pulls into Lorenz's driveway, gets out, walks in and sits down at the dining room table. Lorenz sits down across from Devin, places his drink on a coaster, and slides himself closer to the table.)

LORENZ BURT: All right, Devin I need to explain something to you before we go.

DEVIN COX: You don't have to explain anything, it's cool. I know how to handle myself.
(Lorenz sits there with a very serious look on his face.)

DEVIN COX: What?

LORENZ BURT: This is not a game Devin. If you get in there, and say the wrong thing, they'll kill you right where you stand. And then they'll kill me for bringing you there. Now I need you to listen to me.

DEVIN COX: My fault, I'm listening.

LORENZ BURT: From the very second your feet hit the inside of that building, don't say a word. If they don't ask you a question, you don't talk, no matter what. Now you'll probably get searched three or four times before you even get to the main room, they call it the oval office. They don't trust what they don't know, so always keep your hands in front of you where they can see them. And the most important thing, is your body language. Don't slouch, don't fidget, don't sigh, and please don't look down. Keep eye contact with everybody that talks to you. Now do you understand all of that? If you don't, we need to go over it again. These guys are nothing to mess around with, Devin, I'm serious. I've been involved with these people for a little over four years, and they still scare me to death.

DEVIN COX: I got it.

LORENZ BURT: You sure?

DEVIN COX: I'm good.

LORENZ BURT: I don't want you to be good, I want you to be sure.

DEVIN COX: I'm sure, man.

LORENZ BURT: All right, let's roll.
(As Devin and Lorenz are driving, Lorenz continues to explain to Devin what to do, and what not to do. Once they arrive, as Lorenz said, they're searched three different times. As they walk down the hall towards the oval office, three bodyguards

stop them. The guards stop them by putting the barrel of the guns to each man's chest. Although they've dealt with Lorenz before, they still search them both from head to toe. One bodyguard searches for weapons and microphone wires while the other two press the barrels of their guns to their temples. After the search, the bodyguards let them put their shoes and jackets back on.)

BODYGAURD: I'll give you your wallets and your jewelry back when you leave. When you get inside, don't act stupid, because I will kill you if you do.
(The bodyguard opens the door for them to walk in. Devin can't believe that he's actually going through with this, and at the same time, he realizes that there's no turning back. After walking into the office, the guard shuts the door behind them. In front of Devin and Lorenz, sits a gorgeous twelve-foot long mahogany table. Behind that table, are three huge handmade leather chairs, all turned around with their backs to Devin and Lorenz. The chairs are so big, that you can't tell if anybody is sitting in them when they're facing the other way. Devin and Lorenz look at each other, not really knowing what to do. But one thing they do know, is that they had better not speak. As they stand in confusion and utter fear, the three chairs begin to slowly turn around. The man they call Mr. President, is sitting in the biggest chair in the middle.

 MR. PRESIDENT: Long time no see Lorenz.
(Remembering not to speak unless someone asks him a question, Lorenz doesn't' say a word.)

MR. PRESIDENT: Is this who you put your life on the line for Lorenz?

LORENZ BURT: Yes sir.
(As Devin is shaking in his shoes, Mr. President locks eyes with him and begins a stare down that lasts for five minutes, never saying one word. There is absolute silence in the room. Remembering what Lorenz told him about body language, Devin is horrified to move, or look away.)

 MR. PRESIDENT: You're a cop.
(Knowing that Mr. President is testing Devin to see if he will speak without someone asking him a question, Lorenz very quietly takes a deep breath hoping that he doesn't respond.)

MR. PRESIDENT: I think you're a cop.
(Mr. President slides a sawed off double barrel shotgun out of the hidden holster that's on the side of his chair. He gets up and walks over to Devin with gun in hand.

MR. PRESIDENT: You even look like a cop. That cop look you have, I blasted that same look, right in the face, with this same gun, two years ago. That fool tried to infiltrate my organization undercover. He'd probably be alive today, if I had not had most of his colleagues on my pay roll. The same cops that are always talking about police brotherhood, are the same ones I paid to dime him out. I found him, and I shot him at point blank range just like this.
(Mr. President puts two bullets in the gun, pulls the firing hammers back, and presses it against Devin's forehead.)

MR. PRESIDENT: Now I'm gonna ask you one time. Are you five-0?
(Devin musters up enough phony courage to hold his head high and answer the question.)

DEVIN COX: No sir.

MR. PRESIDENT: Then what is it about you that I don't like, and certainly don't trust?

DEVIN COX: You don't know anything about me sir. That's probably the biggest problem.

MR. PRESIDENT: Are you being smart with me, fool?

DEVIN COX: No sir, not at all. That was an honest answer, sir.

MR. PRESIDENT: I think you're trying to play me. As a matter of fact, get down on your knees.
(Knowing he's being tested, and feeling like he has nothing to lose at this point if Mr. President is really going to shoot him, Devin stands his ground.

MR. PRESIDENT: Turn around and get down on your knees like I told you to.
(He stands face to face with Mr. President.)

MR. PRESIDENT: Nigga I told you to get down on your knees
(Devin doesn't say a word as he tries to keep everything on his body from shaking. Mr. President places the barrels of the gun under Devin's chin.)

MR. PRESIDENT: When you get to hell tonight, tell the other cop I killed that I said hello.
(Even at this point, Devin keeps his mouth shut and stands his ground. Then finally, he gets what he wants. Mr. President asks him a question.)

MR. PRESIDENT: You have any last words before I spread your brains all over the ceiling?
(Devin takes a deep breath, swallows the lump in his throat, and speaks.)

DEVIN COX: If you're gonna kill me, you're gonna have to face me when you do it. I'm not getting down on my knees, and I'm not turning around. I didn't mean any disrespect at all when I answered you. I promise you. I would never do that, especially with a shotgun attached to my forehead and your finger on the trigger.
(Mr. President looks back at his guys, smiles, turns back to Devin, presses the gun against Devin's head, and pulls the trigger. With his mind made up, Devin doesn't even flinch as the hammers click. The only reaction Mr. President got, was the blinking of Devin's eyes.)

MR. PRESIDENT: Were you scared? Did you think I was gonna shoot you?
(Devin is shaking so bad that he can hardly stand up straight.

DEVIN COX: I'm good.
(Mr. President pulls a six-inch switchblade out of his back pocket and slowly rubs it against Devin's cheek.)

MR. PRESIDENT: You good now?
(Feeling a little too full of himself, Devin smiles at Mr. President as if he were calling his bluff. Mr. President smiles back at Devin and then slashes him across his right cheek with the long thin blade. Devin immediately grabs his cheek as blood begins to pour out between his fingers.

MR. PRESIDENT: If I tell you to get on your knees, and turn around, you better do it. Because next time, instead of cuttin' your face, I'm gonna cut your throat, do you understand me? (Devin nods yes which irritates Mr. President to no end. So he grabs Devin by the throat causing blood to come out even more. He then sticks the tip of the blade in Devin right nostril.)

MR. PRESIDENT: Don't nod your head at me, fool, answer my question! Do you understand me?

DEVIN COX: Yes sir.
(Mr. President slowly lets go of his throat, puts the knife back in his pocket, and walks back to his seat.

MR. PRESIDENT: The only reason I didn't kill you, is because of the money you're gonna make for me. I've heard about you, and I know exactly what I'm gonna do with you.
(Devin can't stop shaking as he continues to bleed.)

MR. PRESIDENT: Lorenz, go over there and pour your boy a shot of that Patrone to calm him down.
(Devin slams the shot and puts the glass on the table behind him. Mr. President tells the guy guarding the door to fix Devin's face. So he leaves and comes back with a needle and

medical thread to stitch him up. He pulls up a chair, and sits in front of Devin. Devin sits down, the guard puts on a pair of rubber gloves, and begins to stitch Devin's face. Mr. President's men are all very well trained in many different things.)

MR. PRESIDENT: Devin, explain to me why you're in my office taking up my time.

DEVIN COX: I wanna get paid.

MR. PRESIDENT: So does the rest of America, but they're not in my office wasting my time.

DEVIN COX: The rest of America wants to survive. I don't want to survive, I want to live, and I want to live large. I want to be able to spend on three suits, what most Americans make in a year.

(Mr. President smiles.)

MR. PRESIDENT: "I don't want to survive, I want to live." I like that Devin, I like it, but I don't believe it. You say you want to live, but you walked up in here, almost got yourself shot, and then got half your face sliced up. I know guys in this business that would have had you on a milk carton by morning, if you'd done what you did in this office tonight. The only reason your heart is still beating right now, is because Lorenz seems to think you have something of great value. He said you sell yourself better than anybody he's ever seen. That's a great talent to have, especially in this business, but it's not enough, I need more. Who do you know?

DEVIN COX: Excuse me?

MR. PRESIDENT: I ask you, who do you know? See Devin, running around in the streets selling eight balls and ounces of cocaine are a waste of my time, that's for hustlers. I'm not a hustler, I'm a businessman. What can you bring to the table that I don't already have? I'm always looking to expand my level of clientele. So tell me, who do you know?

DEVIN COX: I know some professional athletes, and some high profile college athletes. I know plenty of college kids, with plenty of their parent's money. I also know some politicians, and I know some of their dirt.

MR. PRESIDENT: Politicians? How do you know any politicians?

DEVIN COX: I sang at the Governor's inauguration a few months ago. At the dinner afterwards, in every conversation I had, I was challenged. They tried to play me to the left to see what kind of mentality I had, and it backfired on every last one of them. They were very impressed when they realized I had a vocabulary, and intellect to go with it. But what really impressed them, was the black skin attached to it. I could talk golf, talk politics, and talk world affairs on their level. I was dressed to impress, I was on, and I was black; they loved me. Since then, I've dined at some of their homes, stayed at some of their beach houses, drank plenty of their fine wines, and

networked myself to death. In other words, I'm in there like swim wear.
(Mr. President leans back in chair and laughs.)

MR. PRESIDENT: Incognito, with your beautiful black self. You know what amazes me about you? How you can sit in that chair, talk as ghetto as you want to, and still not come across as ignorant. You've got it, son; you've got what it takes. You've got all of the tools, and don't know what to do with them. But we're gonna fix that. You will be my greatest work yet. Gentlemen, please stand.
(The two men in the chairs stand up as they're introduced.)

MR. PRESIDENT: Devin, I want you to meet 187. He is my nightmare. If there's a fool out there that tries to shake my business in any way, they're gonna have to deal with 187. Nothing moves through the streets without his permission. Anybody that has ever tried to move weight through the streets without his permission, got missing, and has never been found to this day. You cross him or me, and he'll have you swinging from a tree in your mother's front yard by morning.
(187 sits down.)

MR. PRESIDENT: This is City. City deals with all of my upper class educated clients. The ones that think if you don't make at least three hundred thousand dollars a year, you're a waste of life. That's his area of expertise.
(City sits down.)

MR. PRESIDENT: Devin, these men have been with me for almost twenty years. They're loyal, they do as they're told, they watch my back, and they earn.
(Devin looks at the men.)

MR. PRESIDENT: Devin, before we go any further, I want you to take a trip with 187 down to Louisiana. There's something I want you to see.

DEVIN COX: Sir, again, I don't mean any disrespect, I really don't, and I've learned my lesson. But if at all possible, can it be a weekend trip? It's my senior year of college and I can't afford to miss any of my classes. I've worked too hard to start throwing it all away. I promised my mama that I would go to college and graduate, and I can't let her down.
(Mr. President, who loves his mother more than anything in the world, respects the fact that Devin loves and honors his mom so much. He lets him off the hook for challenging him.)

MR. PRESIDENT: Your mama, ha?

DEVIN COX: She's my world, sir.

MR. PRESIDENT: I understand. There's nothing like mama's love.

DEVIN COX: Nothing in the world, sir.
(As Mr. President sits down, his boys sitting next to him look at each other. They can't believe that he let Devin get away with what he said. They've never seen him take to someone like he's taken to Devin.)

MR. PRESIDENT: Next Friday, when you get out of class, have your bags packed and ready to go.

DEVIN COX: I'll be ready sir.
(Devin and Mr. President lock eyes and smile at each other. In Mr. President, Devin sees what he wants to be. In Devin, Mr. President sees what he wishes he could've been.

SIX

(After an exhausting day of school, Jenna and Joey meet at a little coffee shop near campus. She's been waiting for Joey for almost a half-hour, when he finally shows up.)

JOEY ALLEN: Honey, I'm so sorry I'm late. I was at the library and I lost track of time.
(Joey drops his bag on the floor and sits down.)

JENNA WOODS: It's okay. I'll let you slide this time.
(Jenna smiles as she leans over and gives him a kiss.)

JOEY ALLEN: You're the best.

JENNA WOODS: Tell me something I don't know.
(As Jenna sits back in her chair, she holds on to Joey's hands.)

JENNA WOODS: So how was your day?

JOEY ALLEN: It was good until I remembered that I'm gonna see my parents this weekend.

JENNA WOODS: Yeah but it's your sister's birthday.

JOEY ALLEN: I know.

JENNA WOODS: So what are your parents gonna do for her?

JOEY ALLEN: I'm not sure. I think they may let her have a sleepover.

JENNA WOODS: Well, that'll be fun, she'll love it.

JOEY ALLEN: Yeah, if they don't get drunk and ruin it for her.

JENNA WOODS: Well don't worry about it, we'll be there to run interference if we have to. We'll make sure this is the best birthday she's ever had.

JOEY ALLEN: What would I do without you?

 JENNA WOODS: You won't do anything without me, you're stuck with me forever Mr. Joey Allen.
(Joey, as happy as he's ever been, leans over and gives Jenna a kiss. As the week rolls by, Joey and Devin's apartment becomes more and more weighed down. The intense pressure and stress they're both dealing with is weighing on them. Devin is just one day away from his trip to Louisiana with 187. And Joey is dealing with the fact that in a matter of hours, he'll be home with his parents. He and Jenna have decided to leave on Thursday, instead of Friday, so Jenna can have more time with her parents, and Joey can have more time with his sister Jessica. As Devin and Joey are watching a game, not saying much at all to each other, the phone rings. It's Devin's mom, Mama Lucy.)

DEVIN COX: Hey mama!

LUCY COX: How are you baby?

DEVIN COX: I'm good.

LUCY COX: Are you sure?

DEVIN COX: Yeah I'm fine.

LUCY COX: All right.
(Devin can tell that something is bothering his mother.)

DEVIN COX: Mama, is there something wrong?

LUCY COX: Well, I was hoping you'd tell me. All this week you've been real heavy on my heart, Devin, I've been praying and fasting for you all week long.

DEVINCOX: Mama, you can't do that, you can't go days without eating. You know what Dr. Richardson said about you eating.

LUCY COX: Devin, Dr. Richardson is not Jesus. I need to hear from the Lord about what's going on with you. "Some things come only through fasting and praying." Now if that's what it takes to get what I need from God, then that's just what I have to do. I'm your mother, and I know you better than anybody else in the world. Something's not right somewhere in your life.

DEVIN COX: Mama, everything is fine.

LUCY COX: We'll see. God said he would expose even the secret things we do. You can't hide your life from God, Devin. And you surely won't be able to hide your sin.
(After ten or fifteen minutes of conversation, they hang up the phone. Devin is riddled with guilt, he feels terrible knowing that his selfish decisions have left his mother troubled. But no matter how bad he feels, there's no getting out of the mess he's in. The drug game only has two exits, the prison cell or the grave.)

JOEY ALLEN: Well, I guess I better get on the road.
(Joey grabs his keys and sticks his wallet in his pocket. Devin is so caught up in his guilt, he doesn't even hear Joey talking to him.)

JOEY ALLEN: Yo Devin!
(Devin looks up at him.)

DEVIN COX: What's up?

JOEY ALLEN: What's going on with you? You've been walking around here like a zombie all week. You all right?

DEVIN COX: Yeah I'm straight. I've just got a lot on my mind.

JOEY ALLEN: Anything I can help with?
DEVIN COX: No. I just need to think some things through.

JOEY ALLEN: Well, if you need to talk just call me on my cell phone.

DEVIN COX: I appreciate it, man.
(Devin stands up, tries to give Joey a hug, and Joey stops him as he's done since they were kids. There's just something about hugging another guy that he just doesn't like.)

JOEY ALLEN: Nice try.

DEVIN COX: What is your deal, man? In the twelve years I've known you, you've never hugged me.

JOEY ALLEN: And I'm not going to, so stop trying.

DEVIN COX: All right.
(They shake hands.)

DEVIN COX: I guess I better take what I can get. You guys be careful.

JOEY ALLEN: We will.
(With the car already packed, Joey picks Jenna up, and they hit the road headed for Tennessee on a beautiful North Carolina Fall afternoon.)

SEVEN

(The next day, when Devin gets out of class, he meets 187, they go to the airport, and hop on a plane to Louisiana. Devin is nervous as the thought of him not coming back alive races through his mind. He can't help but think about the fact that he's traveling with a man that kills people for a living and has no remorse. 187 is a code police officers use that means murder.)

DEVIN COX: Are you gonna tell me why we're going to Louisiana?

187: Mr. President wants you to see the rising sun.

DEVIN COX: The rising sun? What is the rising sun?

187: Just relax.
(After their plane lands and they get the rental car, Devin and 187 begin the two hour drive to see the rising sun. With his leg nervously bouncing, Devin tries to just go with the flow, but he can't.)

DEVIN COX: Look, I know you don't want me asking questions, but can you please tell me where we're going?

187: I told you, to see the rising sun.

DEVIN COX: Well, that doesn't help me any.

187: What are you so worried about? You think I brought you all the way down here to kill you or something?
(As Devin turns to look at him, 187 can clearly see the fear in his eyes and begins to laugh.)

187: Devin, if killing you is what I wanted to do, I would have done it by now. I don't need to bring you all the way down here to make you disappear. I'm not gonna kill you.
(Feeling a tiny bit better about the reality he just heard, Devin exhales a quick quiet sigh of relief.)

187: But what I will tell you is this. What we're about to do could cost us our lives, so it's very important that you listen to me. About two miles from here, there's a road that's about twenty miles long that leads to nothing but swamps. That's all that's there. When we get there, at some point, you're gonna see two men with black hoods over their heads come walking out of the woods. Whatever you do, do not look into their eyes, and do not talk to them. I've made this trip only four times in eighteen years, and to this day, this is the part of my job that I hate the most. These two men that are going to come walking out of the woods at some point, I don't know their names, what they look like, who they are, and I don't want to know. If you do anything at all to spook these guys, they will kill us.

They'll cut us up, and they'll throw us in the swamps for the crocodiles, that I do know. These guys we deal with are into all kinds of stuff down here. Voodoo, black magic, casting spells, you name it. As crazy as I am, and as many people as I've killed, you would think that I wouldn't be nervous, but I'm scared out of my mind dealing with these guys. Just their presence alone is almost more than I can handle. What we'll do first, is get into a boat, and travel about ten miles downriver where we'll meet up with three other men. They'll guide us through the woods for about a mile. Once we reach a certain point, we'll walk another half mile on our own.

DEVIN COX: What if we get lost?

187: We won't get lost for two reasons. One, because it's a straight shot from that point. And two, even though we can't see them or hear them, there is always somebody in those woods watching us.
(As they drive down the narrow dirt road to meet the two men, Devin's nerves get the best of him and he again begins to bounce his leg.)

187: Devin, you have got to relax. You can't be all fidgety and nervous around these guys.

DEVIN COX: I can't help it.
(When they finally get there, all they see is a small four man fishing boat with an old rusty outboard motor on the back. 187 parks the car alongside of the little dirt road and turns it off.)

DEVIN COX: Okay. So we have a boat and no guides to drive it. Maybe they forgot we were coming.

187: They didn't forget, they're already here, they're watching us. They're just waiting for us to get out of the car.

DEVIN COX: I don't see anybody.

187: And you won't. Let's go.
(After getting out of the car and walking a few feet, they begin to hear twigs breaking, and leaves crunching. Then all of a sudden, they hear someone running in the woods. Devin nervously looks around as the footsteps get closer, and the sounds get louder. 187 whispers to Devin.)

187: It's them. Remember what I said in the car, do not look at them.

DEVIN COX: I remember.

(As the breaking of twigs and crunching of leaves stop, the sound of gravel being shuffled around begins. Out of the woods, come two sweaty, thin, extremely dark-skinned black men with black hoods over their heads. One of them is wearing an old dingy tee shirt, a dirty pair of camouflage pants, and worn out brown sandals. The other one is wearing a pair of dirty cut off khaki shorts and no shirt. The shorts have several spots of dried blood on the left front leg just above the frayed strings. 187 whispers to Devin.)

187: Just look down at the ground.

(Both Devin and 187 look down as the men slowly approach. The two men not only carry large machete knives, they also carry a very evil presence. With black hoods draped over their heads, all you can see is the whites of their eyes. The two men walk up and stand in front of them. With their heads down, both Devin and 187 can feel the eerie evil presence the two men carry. It surrounds them, sending chills racing up and down their spines. As the smell of deep south sweat and un-bathed bodies fill the air around them, one man grabs Devin's arm, one man grabs 187's arm, and leads them down to the small boat to travel down river. Once they reach their destina-tion, one of the men points, suggesting they get out of the boat. As soon as they step on the muddy bank, the two men turn the boat around and head back up river. Four hours later, Devin and 187 are still standing on the muddy bank as the sun sets, leaving them in the middle of nowhere in complete dark-ness. The swamps are so dark at night, that if you held your hand up one inch from your face, you'd never see it. As they stand on the bank, they hear all sorts of animal sounds they've never heard before. But there's one sound that they hear that sends their hearts racing all over again. They hear the sound of footsteps running and stopping in the woods.)

DEVIN COX: Did you hear that?

187: Shut up and don't say anything.
(Again the footsteps start and stop.)

DEVIN COX: Somebody's out there.
(As soon as Devin gets the word there out of his mouth, two feet land in the mud right behind him. With his heart racing

out of control, and fear consuming every square inch of his mind, Devin's body locks up and he doesn't move. Again, the sound of someone running through the woods starts, except this time it doesn't stop. Three men run out of the woods and stand behind 187. In the pitch dark of night, Devin and 187 stand there with these four men breathing on the back of their heads. They all stand there for about fifteen minutes not saying a word. Unable to see anything at all, both Devin and 187 stand in silence wondering if they're going to die, when all of a sudden, four flash lights are turned on. The lights reveal four black hoods, eight pairs of red eyes, and four very large sharp machetes. When the three men standing behind 187 turn and start walking alongside of the river, the one man standing behind Devin points, letting him know he needs to follow them. When they reach the second destination, one of the men points to his left to let them know which direction they need to go. After walking the half-mile straight through the woods with only a dim flashlight, they come upon a pier that leads to an old rundown shack that sits out on the water. One of the men grabs Devin, and one grabs 187, stopping them in their tracks. Then like a fire shot out of a cannon, for no reason at all, the hooded men turn and take off running through the woods screaming and yelling, sending more chills up and down Devin's spine.)

DEVIN COX: What are they doing?

187: Somebody told me when they do that, they're calling out to all of the dead souls they've cast spells on and buried out here in these woods. You hear that high pitch yelping they're

doing, they're begging those possessed dead souls they've buried out here to meet us in our dreams.
(Devin shakes his head and then looks back at the pier.)

DEVIN COX: Is that a house?

187: No. That's the rising sun.

DEVIN COX: The rising sun is a shack?

187: That's what it looks like on the outside.

DEVIN COX: Okay so what do we do now?

187: We don't do anything. You're on your own from here. I'm not allowed to ever go in again. Even if I could go in, I wouldn't want to.

DEVIN COX: Why not?

187: Just go on inside, Devin.

DEVIN COX: Please come with me.

187: If I go in there with you, they'll kill us both. I told you, I'm not allowed to go back, now go!

DEVIN COX: I don't want to do this.

187: If you refuse to go, you die, President's orders. He told me to kill you myself. Now go!

(Devin takes a deep breath, takes the dim flashlight, and walks out on the pier. When he gets to the door, he turns around looking for 187, and just that fast, he's gone. Devin whispers into the darkness.)

DEVIN COX: Hey! Hey, where are you!
(After calling a second time, the door of the little old shack swings open and two pairs of hands grab Devin. Immediately Devin is slammed down in a chair, tied up, blind folded, and gagged. Standing around him, are several men in black hoods. Some holding knives, some holding guns, and some holding plastic spray bottles with some kind of liquid in them. The man holding the spray bottle walks over, and kneels down in front of him. He pulls Devin's blindfold off.

THE MIST: They call me The Mist. You wanna know why? Because all it takes is a mist of this hydrochloric acid to eat the flesh off of your bones. I enjoy watching this stuff peel skin more than I like looking at a beautiful woman.
(With the Mist's stale smoke breath, and body odor in his face, Devin leans to his left. The Mist grabs him by his neck and sits him up straight. He holds the bottle of acid a quarter of an inch from Devin's nose.)

THE MIST: If you pull away from me one more time, you're gonna find your face dripping onto your lap.
(Behind Devin is an old dusty burlap tarp hanging up in the corner of the little room. Every ten or fifteen seconds, he hears a quiet deep painful murmuring coming from behind the bur-lap tarp. Devin wants so bad to turn and see what's behind the tarp, but he knows it would certainly cost him his life.)

THE MIST: You hear that sound?
(Devin nods yes.)

THE MIST: That's James. James worked for Mr. President at one time. I'm gonna introduce you to James.
(The Mist walks over to the dusty old tarp and pulls it back. Hanging behind that dusty old burlap tarp, is a twenty two-year-old black man that is barely alive. He's covered in blood, he's covered in his own feces, and all of his fingers are missing.)

THE MIST: Now I want you to watch this and watch carefully. If you turn away, or close your eyes, you'll be next.
(The Mist walks over to James, sprays him with the acid, and then walks over to Devin.)

THE MIST: Watch his right knee.
(As the acid soaks in, it begins to liquefy James's skin causing it to fall right off of the bone.)

THE MIST: I love that part.
(The Mist reaches around to his back pocket and pulls out a doll that looks like James. He throws the doll to one of the other men and says something in a language Devin has never heard before. The man walks up to James, pulls a long needle out of his pocket, and sticks it through the dolls stomach causing James to scream at the top of his lungs. After pulling it out, he then sticks it through the middle of the dolls back.
As James screams out, begging for someone to please kill him, Devin begins to cry. He just can't believe what he's seeing.

The Mist walks over to Devin and cuts the rope off of his hands and feet.)

THE MIST: Stand up.
 (Devin stands up.)

THE MIST: Follow me.
(The Mist walks out of the door around to the back of the shack outside on the pier. He waits for the men to bring James out. When they bring him out, they hang the rope that ties his wrist together on a hook at the top of a metal pole.)

THE MIST: Now don't you take your eyes off of him until I tell you to.
(The Mist picks up a bucket full of gasoline, throws it on James, and lights him on fire burning him alive.)

THE MIST: You better watch, or I'll burn you next.
(To save his own life, Devin is forced to watch another human burn alive and scream for mercy. Once he's burned to nothing, they cut him down, throw him in the swamp, and the crocodiles begin to eat his charred remains.)

THE MIST: Leave now and never forget what you've seen here tonight.
(Devin slowly turns and walks the long pier disappearing back into the dark of the Louisiana night. Halfway down the path he sees 187 leaning on a tree waiting for him.)

DEVIN COX: You knew exactly what was going on. Why would you let me go in and see something like that?

187: You needed to know.

DEVIN COX: There is nothing I saw in that house that I needed to know.

187: Yes there was. You needed to know what would happen to you if you ever sold The President short. If money is missing, if product is missing, if you ever try to take more than he wants you to have, it doesn't matter. James was given a certain amount of product, and was expected to return a certain amount of money from that product. The money he returned to us, Mr. President counted it at least ten times, and ten times it came up short.)

DEVIN COX: Is that what this is all about? You guys tortured and killed a man over money?

187: That's the nature of the beast, Devin. At least in this business it is.

DEVIN COX: How much was he short?

187: Six dollars.
(Devin can only shake his head in disbelief.)

DEVIN COX: Six dollars? All of that over six dollars?

187: He didn't do it because of the money, he did it because of the power. When you know that you have the power to say three words, and have something like that done to somebody, you do it because you can. I don't care who you are, when you see one man speak, and make something like that happen, you will fear that man. People respect him out of fear, and that's what he wants. He would rather be feared, than respected.

DEVIN COX: So in other words, he used six dollars as an excuse to feed his ego? That's insane.

187: That's nothing. One day Mr. President was leaving a restaurant and he accidentally pulled out in front of a guy. The guy rolled down his window, gave Mr. President the finger, and told him to go to hell. Mr. President got his plate number, found out where he lived, and before the sun went down that day, I put four bullets right between his eyes, no questions asked. I didn't even know why he wanted the guy killed until the next day. There are strict rules that are set in place by Mr. President. They're rules he's expecting all of us to live by, and anything outside of that is guaranteed to end in death. You're in now Devin, and there's no getting out, not alive. So you better listen, pay attention, and walk the line. And if he asks you to do something, you, without question, better do it.

DEVIN COX: You know what, I just want to get out of here. Get me on a plane and get me out of here.

187: Let's go.
(After the long trek through the woods and the wet dark river ride, Devin and 187 get on a plane and go back to North Carolina with no intentions of ever returning to Louisiana again.)

EIGHT

(Back in Tennessee, it's Saturday morning, and Joey's sister Jessica has turned thirteen years old. It's the day of her big birthday party, and Joey is as excited about all of the fun things they've planned for her as she is. As she peacefully sleeps in her bed, Joey quietly opens the door, tip toes over to the bed, and gives her a light kiss on the cheek. As soon as his lips touch her face, she pops up in a panic.)

JESSICA ALLEN: Don't touch me!
(Startled by her reaction, Joey jumps back and trips over her shoes on the floor behind him.)

JOEY ALLEN: Jessica it's me, it's okay!
(With the blankets tightly gripped in her hands tucked under her chin, Jessica frantically looks around the room. Once she sees that it's Joey that kissed her, she hurries over to him with her heart racing out of control, wraps her arms around him, and holds him as tight as she can. Seeing her panic the way she did, and hearing her scream, "Don't touch me!" gives Joey a clear understanding that something is seriously wrong. After Jessica showers and gets dressed, she comes downstairs to find

all of her favorite breakfast foods sitting on the kitchen table. She also finds her parents wearing party hats and huge smiles.)

BOTH PARENTS: Surprise!
(Jessica's mom gives her a huge hug, a kiss, and hands her a gift.)

JUDY ALLEN: Happy birthday honey, I love you.
(Jessica's dad steps forward and does the same.)

WALTER ALLEN: Happy birthday sweet face, I love you.
(With a huge smile on her face, Jessica sits down at the table and opens her gift. But it's not the gift that's generating that big beautiful smile. It's the fact that her parents are sober, and acting like parents, that's making her happy. That's the only time she can recognize them as loving parents, and not cold-hearted monsters. When they're sober, in Jessica's eyes, they're the epitome of what great parents should be. But when they drink, alcohol isn't the only thing they abuse. With six or seven drinks in them, it's not a matter of will they verbally abuse her, it's a matter of when. Later that same day, Joey's parents take Jessica to her favorite park to have a picnic. As Jessica's mom is pushing her on the swing, Joey and his dad are sitting on a bench watching them.)

WALTER ALLEN: Man, where did the years go? I remember when she was five, she would walk around in those pink rain boots all summer long. No matter how hot it was, she would wear those things and hated to take them off. Now look at her, she's thirteen, she's almost five feet tall, and she's as pretty as they come. I just don't know where all the time went.

JOEY ALLEN: That's what happens when you pass out drunk every day for thirteen years, dad. You miss out on things.
(As Joey gets up to walk away, his dad grabs his arm.)

WALTER ALLEN: You better watch your mouth mister.
(Joey yanks his arm away from his dad.)

JOEY ALLEN: Oh I get it. When I throw the truth in your face, then you become dad. Is that how it works? Is the truth the only thing that can turn you into a responsible parent?

WALTER ALLEN: Do you think you can stop being selfish long enough to let her enjoy her day. Do you have to ruin everything?

JOEY ALLEN: Me ruin her day? Dad, it's great that you want her to have a nice birthday and all, but what about the other three hundred and sixty four days of the year? Why can't you be concerned about her happiness then? Maybe this whole big breakfast, with gifts, and a picnic, is all for you and mom. Is that what this is all about? Is this your way of making up for all of the hell you two put her through when you're drunk?

WALTER ALLEN: Walk away Joey, now. You need to just walk away, before things get out of hand. You're pushing me to close to the edge.

JOEY ALLEN: Yes sir, father. Whatever you say, father.
(Joey walks away leaving his dad steaming mad, and severely convicted. When they get back home, Jessica prepares for her sleepover. She opens the hall closet door and grabs an arm full

of blankets and pillows. As she makes her way down the stairs, blinded by the load she's carrying, Joey turns the corner and runs into her.)

JOEY ALLEN: Oh no! It's the blanket monster!
(Joey tickles Jessica causing her to drop everything. As she slides down the wall laughing hysterically, Joey picks up the pile of pillows and blankets and throws them on top of her. Jessica pops up out of the pile still laughing, only to find Joey gone. He's hiding around the corner.)

JESSICA ALLEN: Where are you?
(When Jessica turns the corner, Joey jumps out, grabs her, and tickles her down to the floor.)

JOEY ALLEN: It's the blanket monster again!
(After turning Jessica three shades of red from laughter, Joey helps her up.)

JOEY ALLEN: Happy birthday kiddo!

JESSICA ALLEN: I'm so glad you came home.
(Jessica gives him a hug.)

JOEY ALLEN: Hey listen, I want to talk to you about something before mom and dad get back from the store.
(Joey grabs Jessica's hand, walks her into the kitchen and sits down at the table.)

JOEY ALLEN: Do you trust me?

JESSICA ALLEN: Yes.

JOEY ALLEN: Do you believe that I would never lie to you?

JESSICA ALLEN: Yes, I do believe that.

JOEY ALLEN: This morning when you were sleeping, and I kissed you, you jumped up and said don't touch me. I've never seen you that scared before Jess.

JESSICA ALLEN: I was having a nightmare and you scared me. (Joey can tell that Jessica's lying.)

JOEY ALLEN: Jessica I'm gonna ask you a question, and I want you tell me the truth all right?
(Jessica nods her head yes.)

JOEY ALLEN: Has anyone ever touched your body against your will?
(With fear draped across her face, Jessica lies to him.)

JESSICA ALLEN: No.

JOEY ALLEN: Has anyone ever tried to get you to touch them on their body in places you shouldn't touch?
(Again she lies.)

JESSICA ALLEN: No.

JOEY ALLEN: You can trust me Jess. I want you to tell me the truth.

JESSICA ALLEN: I am telling you the truth. Can we please not talk about this anymore?
(Seeing that Jessica is uncomfortable, and clearly getting upset, Joey leaves the subject alone for the time being.)

JOEY ALLEN: All right. Give me a hug.
(Joey knows that Jessica has just lied to him. As he holds her tight, he begins to think about what is going on in the house when he's not there. Joey kneels down in front of Jessica, grabs her hand, and looks into her eyes.)

JOEY ALLEN: When I graduate from college, and start making money. I'm gonna buy a house, and you're gonna come live with me.

JESSICA ALLEN: When do you graduate?

JOEY ALLEN: I graduate in May.

JESSICA ALLEN: You promise that you'll come and get me?

JOEY ALLEN: On my life, I promise. Come on, let's take this stuff down stairs.
(Joey and Jessica pick up all of the blankets and pillows and lay out sleeping arrangements downstairs for the big sleep over. Three hours later, with all of Jessica's guests there, and all of them hungry, Joey's parents who should have been back from the store with the food three hours ago, are nowhere to be found. After numerous attempts to reach them on their cell phones, Joey gives up and calls Jenna.)

JOEY ALLEN: Honey, I need you to do me a huge favor.

JENNA WOODS: What is it?

JOEY ALLEN: I need you to go to the store, and pick up some food for Jessica's party. My parents left hours ago to get food and never came back.

JENNA WOODS: You think they're okay?

JOEY ALLEN: I think they're somewhere drunk. I've been calling them for hours.

JENNA WOODS: Well, let's get Jessica straight for right now. What do you need me to buy?

JOEY ALLEN: Just get what you think ten giggly middle school girls would like to eat.

JENNA WOODS: I think I can do that.

JOEY ALLEN: Thank you so much, baby. I owe you big time.

JENNA WOODS: I'll see you soon.
(They hang up the phone and Joey tells the girls the good news.)

JOEY ALLEN: All right ladies, food is on the way!
(Jessica runs up to Joey, hugs his neck, and thanks him for making everything better. An hour after Jenna arrives with the food, and all of the girls are fed, two headlights pull up in the

driveway. Joey looks out of the window, turns around to look at Jenna, and shakes his head in disgust.)

JENNA WOODS: Is it your parents?

JOEY ALLEN: Yeah.
(When Joey looks out of the window for a second time, he sees his parents get out of the car, grab the food they should've had there hours ago, close the car door, and stagger up the driveway.)

JOEY ALLEN: They're drunk.

JENNA WOODS: Let's get all of the girls down stairs.

JOEY ALLEN: You get them downstairs, and I'll deal with these two.

JENNA WOODS: Okay ladies! It's time for makeovers!
(Excited about the makeovers, the girls get up and run downstairs making all sorts of noise. After all of the girls are downstairs, Jessica quickly runs back upstairs to talk to Joey.)

JESSICA ALLEN: If mom and dad are drunk, please don't let them come downstairs.

JOEY ALLEN: Don't you worry about mom and dad. You go on downstairs and have fun with your friends.
(Jessica gives Joey a hug and runs back downstairs. With bags in hand, stale bar smoke in their clothes, and alcohol on their

breaths, Joey's parents stumble through the front door laughing and talking extremely loud. Knowing now is not the time to deal with them because they're drunk, Joey plays Mr. Nice Guy in order to keep the peace.)

JOEY ALLEN: I was starting to get a little worried about you guys!
(Joey takes the bags and puts them on the counter.)

JUDY ALLEN: Joey, I'm going to need you to help me prepare the food for Jessica's party.

JOEY ALLEN: You know what, mom, Jenna and I already took care of it. All of the girls have eaten and they have plenty of snacks down there to nibble on.

WALTER ALLEN: It's about time you do something around here besides eat, sleep, and run up our electricity bill washing your stinking laundry.
(It takes every ounce of patience Joey has to keep him from going off on his dad.)

JOEY ALLEN: You're right, dad, and that's why I wanted to take care of everything on my own. I just wanted to help.

WALTER ALLEN: Well since you're feeling so helpful, make sure you go downstairs and clean up all the mess those girls are going to leave tomorrow, because I'm not!

JOEY ALLEN: I'll take care of everything.

WALTER ALLEN: You better.
(For Jessica's sake, Joey is forced to take every bit of the verbal abuse his dad is throwing at him.)

BETTY ALLEN: Well I at least want to say hello to them before I go to bed.
(Joey's mom starts walking towards the stairs.)

JOEY ALLEN: Mom, you don't want to go down there, you'll embarrass her. You know how kids are at that age. They feel like they can't be cool if their parents are around.

WALTER ALLEN: I can't believe it. The boy finally said something that makes sense. He's right, Judy, you don't need to go down there bothering those kids.

JUDY ALLEN: I guess you're right.
(Judy turns around and follows her husband upstairs to go to bed. When Joey hears their door shut, he leans on the kitchen counter and takes a deep breath. He's so glad that his parents are out of the picture and can't ruin the good time Jessica is having with all of her friends. The next day is Sunday, and it's time for Joey to leave for school. With Jenna waiting in the car, Joey hugs Jessica good bye and whispers in her ear.)

JOEY ALLEN: Remember what I said, don't ever let anybody force you to do anything you don't want to do. You hear me?

JESSICA ALLEN: Yes.

JOEY ALLEN: Here's some money.

(Joey pulls out a fifty-dollar bill.)

JOEY ALLEN: I want you to hide this money somewhere in your room. Now I'm not giving you this money to spend on yourself, I'm giving you this money for emergencies only. If anything ever happens, and you need to leave the house, I want you take this fifty dollars, go across the street to the Hillgrove's, and call Jenna's parents to pick you up. I put their number in your cell phone.

JESSICA ALLEN: I will.

JOEY ALLEN: Give me a hug, I've gotta get going.
(Jessica hugs him as tight as she can.)

JESSICA ALLEN: Don't forget me after you graduate.

JOEY ALLEN: I'll come back and get you.
(Joey gives her a kiss on the cheek.)

JOEY ALLEN: I'll call you from the road.

JESSICA ALLEN: All right.
(After grabbing all of his bags, Joey makes his way out of the door. He throws his things in the trunk, gets in the car, and they drive off. As he waves good bye, his heart yearns for the day when he won't have to leave her there to suffer any more abuse, of any kind, again.)

NINE

(Later on that night when Joey gets home from Tennessee, as he's walking past Devin's door, he can hear Devin talking in his sleep. Joey opens the door and peeks in to make sure he's all right. He finds Devin in a cold sweat slowly rolling back and forth saying, "Don't kill me! Don't kill me!" The next day, around four in the afternoon, Joey is sitting on the couch watching the news when Devin walks in.)

DEVIN COX: What's up, Jo Jo?

JOEY ALLEN: Nothing much. Just recovering from that drive last night, I'm tired.

DEVIN COX: Did you make all of your classes today?

JOEY ALLEN: Barely.
(Devin plops down on the love seat.)

JOEY ALLEN: So why don't you tell me about that dream you had last night?

DEVIN COX: What dream?

JOEY ALLEN: The one that had you sweating and rolling around in your bed saying "please don't kill me."

DEVIN COX: What are you talking about? I slept like a baby.

JOEY ALLEN: Devin, when I got home last night, I heard you talking in your sleep. You were rolling back and forth saying, "Don't kill me," "Don't kill me." Ever since you started hanging out with Lorenz, you've been acting strange man. What's going on?

DEVIN COX: Nothing.

JOEY ALLEN: Are you sure?

DEVIN COX: Yes, I'm sure. Joey, we've been best friends for most of our lives, if something was wrong you know I'd come to you first.

JOEY ALLEN: I would hope so, man. You know I've got your back.

DEVIN COX: You know how we roll Jo Jo. We've been friends a long time, man.
(Devin gets up and walks into the kitchen. He gives Joey a high five as he passes the recliner Joey is sitting in.)

DEVIN COX: Let's go.
(Devin picks up his keys.)

JOEY ALLEN: Go where?

DEVIN COX: I'm taking you out for dinner.

JOEY ALLEN: Devin, it's four fifteen in the afternoon, man.

DEVIN COX: I'm offering you a free meal, and you're arguing with me about it?

JOEY ALLEN: Well since you put it like that, let me grab my shoes.
(Joey puts his shoes on and they head out for dinner. After making their second trip to the buffet, Devin and Joey sit down to grub. As Devin puts the first bite of his juicy steak into his mouth, he looks up and sees a bad situation giving birth to itself. He sees 187 walk in. The last thing Devin wants is for Joey, who is already curious and asking questions, to come face to face with 187. To keep the two of them from running into each other, Devin gets up and goes to the bathroom.)

DEVIN COX: I gotta use the bathroom.

JOEY ALLEN: You just used the bathroom ten minutes ago.

DEVIN COX: It's the soda, man.
(Devin leaves the table and heads for the bathroom, but he doesn't go in. He hides around the corner, and watches 187 to see where he's going to sit. 187 and his friend walk past Devin's table, and turn the corner. Once they turn the corner, Devin can no longer see them or where they're sitting. When Devin finally gets back to his table, he sees 187 sitting only three tables away, diagonally to his left.)

DEVIN COX: Let's go, man.
(Just as Joey scoops up a spoon full of mashed potatoes, he looks up at Devin.)

JOEY ALLEN: What?

DEVIN COX: Let's go, I don't feel good.

JOEY COX: I've only had two plates.

DEVIN COX: Joey, I feel nauseous.

JOEY ALLEN: Can I at least finish this plate?
(Devin sighs.)

DEVIN COX: Just hurry.
(As Devin tells him to hurry, he looks to his left to find 187 staring at him. He motions Devin to come over to his table. Again, Devin is forced to think fast on his feet.)

DEVIN COX: Oh man, there's one of my professors! I'll be right back, I'm gonna say hello.
(Devin walks over to the table and sits down. As they talk, Joey continues to shovel down his food as fast as he can. As 187 is talking, Devin nervously peeks over at Joey. The last thing he wants is for Joey to finish his food and come over to the table.)

187: Devin I'm talking to you.
(Devin quickly turns back to 187.)

DEVIN COX: I'm sorry, what did you say?

(187 looks back at the table where Joey's sitting.)

187: Who's the white boy?

DEVIN COX: He's my roommate.
(Devin looks over at Joey one more time as Joey swallows his last bite of food. Devin instantly goes into panic mode as Joey stands up, leaves a tip, and starts walking towards the table.)

DEVIN COX: Look I really gotta go man. I'll see you tomorrow at the meeting.
(Devin stands up.)

187: I'm not finished talking to you, sit down. What's the big hurry?
(Devin takes a deep breath and sits down as Joey and the life he's secretly living is about to come face to face. Joey walks up to the table and introduces himself)

JOEY ALLEN: How ya doin? I'm Joey Allen.
(Joey extends his hand for 187 to shake and gets nothing. Both 187 and his friend look at each other, and then look at Devin.)

DEVIN COX: This is my roommate Joey.
(187 looks at Joey's extended hand, and then looks Joey in his eyes.)

187: I would tell you where you can stick that hand you've extended to me, white boy, but I'm in a good mood today. So

I'll just tell you this. You've got about three seconds to get your pasty white face away from my table.
(Devin can't believe what he just heard.)

DEVIN COX: Come on man, that's my boy, you don't have to come at him like that.
(187 looks at his friend in shock over Devin's disrespect. His friend can only chuckle.)

187: What did you say?

DEVIN COX: I didn't mean any disrespect, but that's my best friend.
(Joey leans slightly to his right to kind of get between 187 and Devin. He wants to make sure 187 is looking at him when he speaks.)

JOEY ALLEN: Hello, excuse me.
(187 leans back in his chair and crosses his arms.)

JOEY ALLEN: What's your problem?

187: Devin, you better get this fool out of my face.
(As 187 is talking to Devin, he's looking at Joey.)

JOEY ALLEN: You need to relax.
(Joey has no idea he's talking to a man that gets paid to kill. He thinks he's talking to one of Devin's college professors.)

DEVIN COX: Joey, go wait for me in the car.

JOEY ALLEN: I'm not going anywhere.
(Joey and 187 are locked in on each other.)

JOEY ALLEN: Is this how you treat all of your students?
(187's friend gets up out of his seat, walks up to Joey, and stands almost nose to nose.)

187'S FRIEND: You like my new belt, white boy?
(Joey looks down at his belt, but it's not the belt he sees. The man has a black nine millimeter pistol tucked in his waistband. Joey slowly looks at Devin, who is still sitting at the table.)

DEVIN COX: Wait for me in the car, Joey, please.
(Once again, Joey locks eyes with 187's friend.)

187'S FRIEND: Bye bye, little Joey.
(When Joey turns to walk away, he makes eye contact with 187. He lifts his hand up to show Joey just how close he came to getting shot. He holds his index finger and thumb less than a quarter of an inch apart.)

187: This close, white boy. You came this close.
(Joey walks away leaving Devin in some serious trouble. After he's gone, both 187 and his friend sit down and immediately lock in on Devin.)

187: You've got two minutes to save his life. If you don't explain what just happened, you'll be putting what's left of him in the ground next week.

DEVIN COX: He's my best friend, we grew up together. He's like a brother to me.
(187 takes a deep breath.)

187: It's not gonna work Devin. Rolling with that white boy is not gonna work. He's bad for business. He's a hot head. He's gonna get you in trouble, and when you get in trouble, you run the risk of us getting in trouble. There are two things we don't do. We don't take risks and we don't take white people. We'll take their money, but not them.

DEVIN COX: He doesn't know anything about you, or what I'm doing. There's nothing to worry about.

187: Oh I'm not worried, but you should be. You see Devin, Mr. President does not do white. And because he doesn't do white, we don't do white. You included.

DEVIN COX: I told you he doesn't know anything. And besides, Mr. President doesn't have to know anything about him.

187: We don't get down like that. When trouble comes, we sound the alarm. I'm telling you now, your boy out there is trouble. I should drop two hot ones in him.

DEVIN COX: Joey is not trouble.

187: He's trouble for you. Because when I inform Mr. President of this, he's gonna deal with that madness you got goin on.

DEVIN COX: As long as Joey doesn't know what we do, why is it a problem?

187: It's a problem because he's white, and they cannot be trusted, none of them. They don't trust us, and we don't trust them. I don't care how much he smiles in your face, If it came down to it, he would sell you out, call you a nigga, and turn on you faster than you can blink your eyes. You can't trust them Devin. You're in college, read your history books.

DEVIN COX: History? Did you know that black people owned slaves? We purchased and sold our own people. That's a historical fact.

187: Devin, your little classroom facts don't mean a thing to me. I know what I know. They cannot be trusted.

DEVIN COX: How can you sit here and try and school me about not trusting white people, and you kill black folks for a living?

187: I'm gonna let that one slide. I've killed people for less than that, so you better watch your mouth.

DEVIN COX: So what you're telling me, is that I have to cut off everybody in my life that's not black?

187: No I am not telling you that. But Mr. President is going to tell you that. No risk, no ruin. That's his favorite saying.

DEVIN COX: Well, then I want out. I'm not gonna blow off all of the people I love man, I'm not doing it.
(187 looks at his friend and smiles. His friend looks at Devin and shakes his head.)

187'S FRIEND: For a college boy, you sure are stupid.

187: There is no out Devin, we own you. When you walked into the oval office, you crossed the line in the sand. You're on the road to nowhere. You can never get out. Now I suggest you leave, before that fool comes back in here and makes me kill him.
(It's so funny how the choices we make now, can dictate the life we have later. Devin walked into a restaurant looking for a good meal. But instead, he found his future soul mate, and her name is regret. She's a woman that will control his every waking moment. She'll rob him of the little peace of mind he has left. She'll create realities that really don't exist. And eventually, she'll be the one to hand Devin his invitation to an early grave. When Devin gets in the car, Joey immediately begins to question him.)

JOEY ALLEN: So that was one of your professors, huh? What class does he teach, how to commit the perfect hate crime? Tell me who he really is, and why you're keeping company with guys that carry nine-millimeter pistols.
(Not wanting Joey to know the truth, Devin lies. The mindset and quick tongue of a hustler, has replaced the morally good foundation that made Devin who he truly was.)

DEVIN COX: It's not like that, Joey. I don't keep company with either one of those guys. The guy that got in your face, is an undercover cop. The other guy, is one of those militant black radicals that hates anything that's not black. He organizes rallies and protests at my school.

JOEY ALLEN: Why did you lie to me?

DEVIN COX: What did you expect me to say? Hey, Joey, don't come over to the table, they hate white people.

JOEY ALLEN: I expect you to tell me the truth Devin, best friends remember? How do you know them?

DEVIN COX: I met them on campus. Look, I'm sorry man, I'm sorry I lied to you.
(Devin reaches out to shake Joey's hand to make peace.)

JOEY ALLEN: Next time, just tell me the truth?
(Joey shakes his hand.)

DEVIN COX: I'll never lie to you again.
(With a lying smile on his face, Devin gives Joey a handshake of deceit. The once dedicated friend-to-the-end Joey once had, has now become the very monster he'll soon have to destroy.)

TEN

(Back in Tennessee, Joey's parents have been on a two-day drinking binge. They started on Friday when they got off of work, and drank all day Saturday. It's now three a.m. Sunday morning and they are passed out cold. As Joey's sister Jessica peacefully sleeps in her bed, a sliver of light from the hallway interrupts the darkness in her room. Their next door neighbor, Paul, who drinks with her parents, has a key to their house. He and his wife take care of their cats when they're out of town. Paul, buying liquor, and bringing it over to Joey's house isn't a nice gesture, it's a tool. He drinks with them, gets them falling down drunk, and then comes back at two or three in the morning. He unlocks the door, walks into Jessica's room, lays down next to her, and sexually abuses her. This sick twisted abuse started the weekend after Joey left for college. That's why Jessica jumped up screaming out of her sleep the morning of her birthday when Joey kissed her on the cheek. The next morning, as Jessica and her parents are sitting at the table having breakfast, they hit Jessica with a bomb.)

WALTER ALLEN: Jessica, next weekend your mother and I are going out of town. Some friends of ours from college are renewing their wedding vows, it's their thirty-year wedding

anniversary. Paul and Nancy next door said it was all right if you stayed with them.
(Knowing what she's in for if she stays next door where Paul lives, Jessica instantly begins to search for a way of escape.)

JESSICA ALLEN: Why can't I call Joey? If he came home I could stay here.

WALTER ALLEN: Joey's in another state. He can't just pick up and come home anytime he wants. You don't want to stay with the Millers?

JESSICA ALLEN: No.

JUDY ALLEN: Why not?
(Jessica wants so bad to tell them what's been going on. But Paul Miller, over time, has lied and deceived her into thinking that her being molested by him is her fault. He lied and told her that if she said anything, her parents would have her committed to a youth facility for troubled teens. He also convinced her that her parents would never believe her word over another adults; and that he would tell her parents that he saw her doing drugs with some other kids in the neighborhood. He used an adult mind, to deceive childish eyes. She sees every threat he's ever made to be absolute truth.)

JESSICA ALLEN: I want to stay home and sleep in my own bed.

JUDY ALLEN: Well you're not staying here by yourself, so you may as well accept what we're telling you. You're staying at the Millers', and that's that.

(Now completely upset, Jessica gets up and goes to her room.)

WALTER ALLEN: And we don't want to hear any more about it either!

(As the week goes on, Jessica spends every waking moment worried and stressed out about staying at the Millers'. She knows the mental, emotional, and physical torment that awaits her. But sadly enough, there's nothing she can do about it. Finally, Friday arrives, her parents go out of town, they leave her at the Millers', and the suffering repeats its evil cycle.)

ELEVEN

(Back in Raleigh, Devin has just sat down with Mr. President. He can clearly see that Mr. President is not happy with him.)

MR. PRESIDENT: I've been contemplating for days whether or not I should have that white boy killed. Three days in a row, I sent 187 out to lay him to rest, and changed my mind every time. The only reason he's still alive, is because I've got one of the biggest deals I've ever done coming up in the next two weeks, and I don't want any distractions or problems. I don't want anybody in my camp making waves right now.

DEVIN COX: Mr. President, what happened at the restaurant was my fault. Joey didn't know who he was dealing with. I told him that 187 was one of my professors. He's not a bad guy.

MR. PRESIDENT: Devin, the organization I run is an all-black organization. When it comes to white folks, we use them as customers, not confidants. We don't do white around here. They're only good for pay, not pleasure, not even the women. There is no getting involved with white people in this family. Now, I don't know what the deal is with you and this white boy, and I don't care. But this whole hanging out, kickin' it thing you're doing with him, is gonna have to stop.

DEVIN COX: Can I please explain something?

MR. PRESIDENT: You can, but it won't do you any good.

DEVIN COX: Joey and I have been best friends since we were eight years old. I've been through a lot of hell in my life, and he's been there every step of the way. When my father died, that was the hardest thing I've ever had to deal with. I can honestly say, that if Joey had not been there, I might still be battling depression.

(The other guys sitting in on the meeting are looking at each other somewhat confused. They can't believe that Mr. President is allowing Devin to respond to what he has said is his final decision. They've seen him kill a person for the very thing Devin is getting away with. In their eyes, Devin is blatantly challenging Mr. President's authority. They're seeing that Mr. President's connection to Devin has crossed over from business, to personal. For most of them, this new behavior is creating a nervous environment. But for one in particular, it creates an extreme amount of jealousy. They all think bringing Devin in is going to be bad for business.)

MR. PRESIDENT: Devin, let me give you a little scenario. Let's just say I sent you and one of the guys out to handle something for me and your little white friend just happened to show up. Now it's obvious that your boy has got some heart, he proved that. I can respect that, but I won't tolerate it. If he were to ever interfere with my business, he would go see the rising sun.

(Devin lets out a deep sigh of stress.)

MR. PRESIDENT: And when you go see the rising sun, you don't come back from the rising sun. So you need to do what you have to do to fix this little situation you have. He won't get away twice.

DEVIN COX: Yes, sir. You have my word that it will never happen again, I promise. If it does I'll take the heat.

MR. PRESIDENT: Wrong answer. You won't take the heat. You'll take the same trip he takes, and you won't come back either.

(Devin can see in Mr. President's eyes that what he just said was not a threat, it was a promise.)

MR. PRESIDENT: You said you graduate in May, right?

DEVIN COX: Yes, sir.

MR. PRESIDENT: The day you graduate, I want you to move out of that apartment. I don't want you living with that white boy when you start handling my business.

DEVIN COX: I won't be able to afford it, I can barely pay my bills now.

MR. PRESIDENT: You don't need to concern yourself with that. Your bills, your place to live, your ride, it'll all be taken care of. The only thing you need to do is focus on handling my business, you understand?

DEVIN COX: Yes, sir.

MR. PRESIDENT: How much is your rent?

DEVIN COX: My half is four hundred a month.
(Mr. President turns his right hand upside down and taps his pinkie ring on the table. That's his way of telling the man that handles all of the money that he wants money on the table right now.)

MR. PRESIDENT: Hook him up.
(Once again, the other guys are shocked. They just can't believe what they're seeing. The man pulls a thick money roll out of a little gray box under the table without hesitation. He gives Devin four hundred dollars.)

MR. PRESIDENT: Now that's not night-out-on-the-town money, that's pay your rent money. Don't blow it.

DEVIN COX: Yes, sir, thanks.

MR. PRESIDENT: Don't thank me, just do what I told you to do.

DEVIN COX: I will.

MR. PRESIDENT: Go on home and study.

DEVIN COX: Yes sir.
(Devin gets up and walks out of the office. After he leaves, the guys all look at each other. City, his number one right hand man, stands up.)

CITY: Fellows, can you give us a few minutes alone please?
(The guys all get up and leave the room. Once they're all gone, City turns his chair towards Mr. President to face him.)

MR. PRESIDENT: What's up?

CITY: What's going on with you man?

MR. PRESIDENT: What do you mean?

CITY: With this kid Devin. I've been with you for over twenty-five years, longer than anybody else here. We've been friends since we were twelve. I've never seen you negotiate with anybody, it's always been your way or no way.
(Mr. President laughs.)

CITY: I'm serious, man. You've had people killed for far less than what he just did. Help me understand what's going on. Because, me, I've got a bad feeling about this kid Devin, I smell trouble.

MR. PRESIDENT: You getting paranoid on me, man?

CITY: The last four times I thought I smelled trouble I was right. I've never stolen a dime from you, I've never sold you short in any way, and I've never given you bad advice. Listen to what I'm saying to you. We need to get rid of him, and we need to get rid of him now. I've got a bad feeling on this one.

MR. PRESIDENT: Follow me.
(Mr. President gets up and walks over to the fully stocked bar on the other side of his office. Once they reach the bar, Mr. President pulls out an unopened bottle of twenty-year-old scotch, and two glasses.)

MR. PRESIDENT: Have a drink with your friend.

CITY: Come on, man, I'm serious. We need to talk about this.

MR. PRESIDENT: I know you're serious and that's the problem, you're always serious. You don't know how to relax man. Yes, you have always watched my back, and for that I'm grateful, you know I am. I appreciate everything you've done to help me get to where I am. I couldn't have done it without you. But with Devin, I know what I'm doing. I promise you. I'm telling you, this kid is the real deal, man. He's got so much of what it takes to succeed in what we do, that it's almost scary. He's only twenty years old, and mentally, he's so far ahead of the game. So you just relax, take it easy, and trust me on this one, all right?
(Mr. President hands him his glass of scotch.)

CITY: It's your call.

MR. PRESIDENT: A toast.
(They both raise their glasses.)

MR. PRESIDENT: To friendship, to loyalty, and to success. May they continue to create for us an indestructible power, to control the drug game from here, to hell and back.
(They tap their glasses together and drink. After they're done, they set their glasses on the bar. Mr. President puts his hands on City's shoulders as they stand there in silence looking at each other. Mr. President takes a deep breath.)

MR. PRESIDENT: Would you die for me?
(City pauses for a few seconds and then answers.)

CITY: Yes, I would.
(Mr. President wraps his arms around City and holds him tight. City responds by hugging him back. In City's mind, the bond they've had for the last twenty-five years has just been strengthened by the embrace. But, in Mr. President's eyes, the first crack in the bond has now revealed itself. Asking City if he would die for him was not a question of loyalty; it was a cold warning of what is soon going to be the darkest day of his life.)

TWELVE

(It's now Friday, May 5th, and graduation is less than 24 hours away. Joey, Jenna, and Devin are hanging out at Joey and Devin's apartment. Both Joey and Jenna know that Devin is moving out the first week after graduation. While their parents and other invited guests are resting from the drive into town at their hotels, the three of them decide to cut loose one last night, before walking away from the only world they've known for the last four years.)

DEVIN COX: Well, this is it, our last night as college students.

JOEY ALLEN: Can you believe that we're actually graduating tomorrow?

JENNA WOODS: No, I can't.

DEVIN COX: Well, let's not waste valuable drinking time, let's roll out.

JOEY ALLEN: I want to stop at my parent's hotel on the way to check on Jessica.

DEVIN COX: We'll catch a cab from their hotel, because none of us are driving tonight. Tonight, it's all out.

JENNA WOODS: We'll drive my car and park it at my friend's sorority house. The Wolf's Den is just around the corner. We'll call a cab to get back home.

DEVIN COX: There it is! That's the game plan, now let's go!

JOEY ALLEN: Baby, you don't mind stopping at my parents' hotel do you?

JENNA WOODS: Not at all.

DEVIN COX: Hey, Bonnie and Clyde, can we please go party? You guys are flowing like molasses!

JENNA WOODS: Shut up, you're just jealous.

DEVIN COX: Yeah, whatever.
(They walk out with Joey locking the door behind him. When they get to the hotel where Joey's parents are staying, they all decide to go up and see Jessica. After getting off of the elevator and walking about fifteen or twenty feet, they begin to hear a murmuring cry. As they get closer to his parent's room, the sound gets louder.)

JOEY ALLEN: That sounds like Jessica.
(They reach the room, and can clearly hear that it is Jessica. Joey pounds on the door with his fist and screams her name. Jessica responds by screaming "Help me Joey." Joey begins to

kick the door as hard as he can. After the fourth kick the door flies open, and what they find is an absolute shock to them all. They find Joey's neighbor, Paul Miller, scrambling to gather his things. He had taken his shirt, tie, and shoes off. Both he and his wife were invited to the graduation by Joey's parents, but his wife couldn't make it. Joey's parents are nowhere to be found, they were down in the hotel bar drinking. Paul Miller was drinking with them, but he told them he was going to turn in early and get some rest. They asked Paul to check in on Jessica from time to time to make sure she was okay. But instead of keeping her safe, he decided to keep her in torment by attempting to molest her once again. As Joey stands there fuming in complete shock, Jenna walks over to the bed and hugs Jessica. She grabs the bed sheet and wraps it around Jessica as she cries hysterically.)

JENNA WOODS: What did you do to her?
(Joey grabs the lamp off of the table, and breaks it over Paul Miller's head. Then, as if it was a fight for life or death, Joey attacks Paul and the fight is on as Joey repeatedly screams.)

JOEY ALLEN: I'm gonna kill you!

DEVIN COX: Jenna, you have a key to our apartment, take Jessica to our place!
(After Jenna and Jessica leave the room Devin grabs Joey to stop him, but has no success. All of the commotion has caused people up and down the hall to come out of their rooms. When the man that's staying directly across the hall walks out and sees what's going on, he runs into the room to lend Devin a hand, but has no success. Completely enraged, Joey slings both

of them off of his back, and continues to pound on Paul Miller's face. The hotel security guard that happens to be six foot five, two hundred and thirty pounds, comes barreling into the room and grabs Joey. Even with the guard's strength, and size, both Devin and the other guest still have to help. Once they have Joey under control, the police show up. They put Joey and Paul Miller in handcuffs, put them in separate cars, and take them to the police station. After questioning everybody that witnessed what happened, the magistrate sets a 3,000-dollar bond for Joey. He's been charged with assault, destruction of private property, resisting arrest, and a couple of other things. It's only three thousand dollars because he has a clean record. In the state of North Carolina, only fifteen percent of that bond is necessary. So Devin runs to the ATM, grabs four hundred and fifty dollars, and pays the bail bondsman to get him out. Once that's all settled and they're walking out of the station, they're met by a couple of reporters and camera men. Television stations have police scanners, and are able to hear what's going on. As Joey is walking, trying to avoid the reporters and the cameras, he realizes that they're not going to go away.)

JOEY ALLEN: I have nothing to say! Can you please get that camera out of my face?
(Devin pushes the camera away to get it out of Joey's face. In the process of doing so, they get a straight on shot of his face instead. One hour later, at 10:55p.m. during a commercial, the anchorman for channel five news comes on to talk about the top stories coming up on the eleven o'clock news.)

ANCHORMAN: I'm Jason Benson and here are our top stories coming up at eleven. At a local hotel, occupied by out of town

guests here for college graduation tomorrow, the possible molestation of a young girl ends in a brutal and bloody attack.
(At that time, Mr. President's right hand man, City, who is sitting at his desk at home doing some paper work, stops what he's doing to listen to the anchorman. Hearing the anchorman talk about a little girl being molested upsets him.)

CITY: Sick pervert. If he's guilty I hope they fry him.
(Just as he finishes his sentence, he sees footage of Devin walking out of a police station, shoving a cameraman's camera out of his face.)

CITY: No! No! No!
(City walks over to the television to get a closer look. He shakes his head and talks to himself.)

CITY: I knew it! I knew he was trouble!
(He immediately gets on the phone and calls Mr. President.)

MR. PRESIDENT: It's eleven o'clock at night. I hope this is important.

CITY: Did I, or did I not tell you, that Devin was trouble?

MR. PRESIDENT: What are you talking about, man?

CITY: I just saw that fool walking out of a police station on T.V.

MR. PRESIDENT: A police station! What was he doing at a police station?

CITY: I don't know. They were talking about some young girl being molested, and then they showed him and that white boy walking out of the police station. He was actin' like a fool, shoving the cameraman's camera around.
(Mr. President takes a deep breath as his blood begins to boil.)

MR. PRESIDENT: I want you to call him, and tell him, that if he is not in my office in the next forty-five minutes, he's a dead man! If you can't get in touch with him, call me back, and I'll send 187 to go find him.

CITY: Maybe we should just cut our losses and get rid of him. If he molested that little girl, he could dime us out to cover his own tail?

MR. PRESIDENT: I don't want to do anything until I find out what's goin' on.

CITY: Did you hear anything I just said to you, man? He was on T.V. coming out of a police station. We don't need that kind of attention.
(For the second time, City has questioned Mr. President's decision and authority. This type of behavior in Mr. President's eyes is a serious sign of trouble.)

MR. PRESIDENT: You know what never mind, I'll get 187 to find Devin. I want you to meet me at my office.

CITY: For what?
(Mr. President hangs up on him. When City gets to the office he walks in and sits down in front of Mr. President.)

MR. PRESIDENT: Stand up.
(Both City and Mr. President stand up putting them only inches apart.)

MR. PRESIDENT: Now back up off me.
(City takes two steps back.)

MR. PRESIDENT: What's your problem? And keep in mind that I'm in a bad mood.

CITY: I think we're getting ready to see some bad days, baby, real bad. You're trying to turn a middle class, uppity mama's boy, into a drug hustler, and it's not gonna work. He's an immature kid, not a kingpin. You're trying to create another version of you, and it's gonna cost us everything. These people we deal with, they've been doing this for a long time, man. They are going to spot every weakness he has, and they are going to eat him alive. His weakness is a direct reflection of you, and how we do business. You don't want that. People respect you, because they know there is no weakness. No weakness, and no mercy, that's our reputation. Devin ain't hood man. He ain't hood. Anybody that will come in here, knowing what we do, and say things like, "I promised my mama," is a wrong candidate for our organization. He's soft, and you know it as well as I do. In this business, sensitivity does not survive. He's gonna get us busted, or he's gonna get us all killed.

MR. PRESIDENT: So he's all wrong for us you think?

CITY: No I don't think he is, I know he is.

(Mr. President walks over to the bar, pours himself a drink, and sits down in his chair.)

MR. PRESIDENT: In all the years I've known you, I've never seen you so bothered by any one person.

CITY: I don't like him, and I don't like his vibe.

MR. PRESIDENT: Let me ask you something. Are you jealous of him? Or, are you afraid of him?
(City sits down, leans back in the chair, clasps his hands together, and smiles at Mr. President. After about ten seconds of silence, he answers his question.)

CITY: So it's like that now?
(Mr. President takes a sip of his drink and then puts the glass on the table.)

MR. PRESIDENT: You tell me. You're the one, the only one, running around here banging on the panic button. You're a money guy. That's what you do. You take care of my money and the business side of what I do, and you're good at it. So if it's you losing your position that's got you acting all crazy, you can relax, I would never replace you. You'll always be my vice president. But Devin, he stays.

CITY: What about this molestation thing?
(There's a knock on the door.)

MR. PRESIDENT: Yeah!
(The man guarding the door peeks his head in.)

GUARD: Mr. President, 187 is out here with Devin.
(Mr. President and City look at each other.)

MR. PRESIDENT: Send them in.
(Devin comes through the door first with 187 holding him by the back of the neck.)

DEVIN COX: I can explain everything!

MR. PRESIDENT: I appreciate you finding him.

187: You want me to stay?

MR. PRESIDENT: Give us a few minutes.
(187 waits out in the hall.)

DEVIN COX: I promise you it's not what you think it is!

CITY: No it's exactly what we think it is. We think we saw you on T.V. walking out of a police station.

DEVIN COX: But I didn't do anything!

CITY: Then why were you coming out of a...
(Mr. President cuts City off in mid-sentence. He can't believe that Mr. President would embarrass, and belittle him, especially in front of Devin.)

MR. PRESIDENT: I need you step out of the room and leave us alone.
(City leans forward on the table.)

CITY: I don't think that's a good…
(Upset that City didn't follow his orders immediately, Mr. President stands up, cuts him off in mid-sentence, and yells.)

MR. PRESIDENT: Nigga, get up out of my office! Now!
(City gets up and walks out slamming the door behind him. Mr. President sits back down.)

MR. PRESIDENT: I'm in a fit of rage, I'm tired, and I really want to kill you right now, Devin. Time is not on your side, so you need to quickly give me a reason not to call 187 in here and cut your throat. I mean quick.

DEVIN COX: First of all, I wasn't arrested. When Joey and I got to his parent's hotel, where they're staying for graduation, we found a man trying to rape his little sister. Joey jumped on him, gave him a beat down, the cops came, they threw him in jail, and I bailed him out. When we were coming out of the police station, that's when the television cameras got us. And to be honest with you, I don't blame Joey. I would have tried to kill him too if it were my sister.

MR. PRESIDENT: Oh, you would've killed him, huh tough guy?

DEVIN COX: Right there on the spot.

MR. PRESIDENT: Let me give you a little advice, Stupid. Distance is the hand sanitizer that will keep your hands the cleanest. Out of sight, out of mind.

DEVIN COX: I understand.

MR. PRESIDENT: Not one drug user I've sold drugs to, has ever seen my face. And, they've made me stinking rich. None of the people that have traded their money, for my poison, even know I exist. Out of sight, out of mind. They can't tie me to anything.

DEVIN COX: I get it, sir.

MR. PRESIDENT: Go home and start packing your stuff.

DEVIN COX: Packing for what?

MR. PRESIDENT: Tomorrow, I'm moving you into your own condo.

DEVIN COX: Are you serious?

MR. PRESIDENT: Do I look like I'm serious?

DEVIN COX: Oh man, my own place. I can't believe it, a condo for real?
(Devin is so excited.)

MR. PRESIDENT: For real.
(Seeing Devin's excitement makes Mr. President smile. Mr. President then reaches into his desk drawer and pulls out five thousand dollars.)

MR. PRESIDENT: Congratulations.
(He hands Devin the money. Devin's mouth is wide open but nothing is coming out.)

MR. PRESIDENT: That's your graduation present. Just a little something to get you started in life.
(Mr. President walks around the table and stands in front of Devin.)

MR. PRESIDENT: Stand up.
(Devin stands up and he and Mr. President are face to face.)

MR. PRESIDENT: Son, if you listen to me, work hard for me, and stay loyal to me, that five thousand dollars, is just the beginning of what I'll give you. I will make you a king, Devin, The king of your own world.
(Devin is now starting to distort the difference between crime figure, and father figure. He's starting to look at Mr. President as a role model, instead of the monster he really is. He looks Mr. President directly in the eyes.)

DEVIN COX: I'll never disappoint you if you give me the opportunity to prove myself. You'll see in time, that I am, and always will be, your greatest asset. Not one of those guys that work for you, will ever come close to achieving what I'm about to do. They're beneath me, I'm that sure of myself.

MR. PRESIDENT: Take it easy, don't go there. There's a whole lot you need to learn, and they're the ones that are going to teach you. So don't disregard those guys, and don't ever disrespect them. They're loyal to me. But I wouldn't put it past them to act on their own if you cross them. They can make you disappear and deny ever having anything to do with it, be mindful of that. I believe in you, Devin, and I see more potential in you at the age of 22, than I see in all those guys put together. But that's all it is at this point, it's just potential. You still don't know anything about what we do, and how it's done.

DEVIN COX: You're right.

MR. PRESIDENT: I'm always right.
(Devin smiles.)

MR. PRESIDENT: Go on home. You've got to get up in the morning, and make your mama proud.

DEVIN COX: Thanks again for everything, I really do appreciate what you've done.

MR. PRESIDENT: Go on home.
(Mr. President shakes Devin's right hand, and wraps his left arm around him at the same time.)

DEVIN COX: I'll see you on Monday.

MR. PRESIDENT: Eight a.m. sharp.

DEVIN COX: Yes sir.
(As Devin is walking towards the door to leave, Mr. President can only smile. In Devin, he not only sees a lucrative cash cow. He also sees the son he's always wanted.)

THIRTEEN

(With a crisp chill in the air, and a light dusting of snow on the ground, the month of December is ushered in. Six months have now passed, and Joey's parents have become more reckless than ever. Feeling completely responsible for what happened to their daughter, Walter and Judy Allen are drinking five days a week. They've gotten so out of control that Judy Allen not only lost her job, but she's facing possible jail time for a third DWI. She's gotten three in four months. Walter Allen is drinking excessively to deal with his pain and guilt. He's starting to depend more and more on Oxycodone, and Xanax, to get him through each day. But it's been Jessica that's had the biggest change in behavior and personality. Every waking moment of her life, she's battling the spirit of deception. She's being deceived by the shame, the self-doubt, feeling worthless, depressed, angry, and extremely revengeful. But the most deceptive spirit of them all, is the one that's constantly trying to convince her to just end it all. She believes that all of the awful things Paul Miller did to her is her fault. In her head, she hears his violent voice whispering to her over and over again. The voice whispers, "What do you expect a man to do when you dress like that?" "If you didn't act like you do, none of this would be happening." "This is what happens to girls like you." This sweet, innocent, thirteen year-old child, now feels complete responsibility for the abuse, and the fall out because of it. With her heart now turned to stone, Jessica has begun her own little routine of masking pain. She's gone from wearing what is appropriate for a thirteen-year-old, to short, tight skirts, low-cut shirts with her stomach also showing, somewhat heavy make-up, and an extremely, outgoing flirty personality. She's hanging out with the party crowd. She's smoking, drinking, and she's gone from straight A's, to barely making D's. She's been suspended twice for fighting, once for smoking on campus, and once for skipping classes. Her parents are aware of what's going on with her, but because of the guilt they feel, they've chosen to deal with her like they're her friends instead of her parents. They pretty much let her do whatever she wants, if they think it's going to make her happy. That's their way of saying "I'm sorry." That's their way of making everything right. They think they're making her happy by letting her run wild, but what they are really doing, is loading the scales so that she may never live to see the age of fourteen. Back in North Carolina, Joey is preparing to do something that he's had in the works for months. For six months now, Joey, along with a lawyer, and child protective services in Tennessee, have been keeping a close eye on his parents, their activities, Jessica, her activities, and the condition of her home life. They feel they have enough evidence to prove without a shadow of a doubt that Jessica is living in an unsafe environment that is detrimental to her well-being. So Joey, Jenna, and Joey's lawyer, are on their way to Tennessee to meet the child protection service caseworker and the Loudell police to remove Jessica from his parent's home. Joey is taking Jessica back to North Carolina, and taking his parents to court for full custody.

Because Joey always had a good reputation growing up in Loudell, and was considered a good role model for younger kids, he's got a lot of people in Loudell standing behind him to back him up. It's a Friday evening, around 7:30p.m., and his parents are well on their way to another night of intoxication. Jessica is sitting out back on the deck having a smoke with a couple of her friends, when there's a knock on the door. Joey's dad, Walter stands up, stumbles towards the door, and opens it only to find a child protection service agent's badge, and a search warrant staring him in the face.)

AGENT OSBORNE: Walter Allen.
(Walter's eyes grow wide as he looks at all of the familiar faces staring at him.)

WALTER ALLEN: What is all of this?
(At that moment, a face that Walter does recognize, steps out from behind a blue police uniform. It's Joey.)

JOEY ALLEN: They're with me, and I'm here for Jessica. Where is she?
(Walter can't believe it. He locks his eyes in on Joey.)

WALTER ALLEN: Are you stupid bringing all of these people here?

AGENT OSBORNE: Mr. Allen, my name is Sara Osborne. I'm a retrieval agent for child protective services and I'm here to remove Jessica Allen from your home.
(Walter ignores the agent, her badge, and locks in on Joey again.)

WALTER ALLEN: Do you really think I'm gonna let you just waltz in here and take my daughter?

JOEY ALLEN: You don't have a choice. Now where is she?
(Walter Allen lunges forward and goes straight for Joey's throat.)

WALTER ALLEN: I'll beat your brains out!
(The police officer grabs Walter, takes him down to the ground, and cuffs him.)

POLICE: Mr. Allen you're under arrest for attempted assault and communicating threats.
(Walter continues to squirm and scream, wishing he could get his hands on Joey.)

AGENT OSBORNE: Let's go.
(With the agent leading the way, they walk in the house to find Jessica. As they round the corner, they're met with even more opposition. Betty Allen, Joey's mom, tries to stop them.)

JOEY ALLEN: Mom, sit down and stay out of the way! I'm here to get Jessica! She's coming to live with me!
(The other police officer stands in front of Judy Allen.)

POLICE: Ma'am you can sit down, or you can go to jail, it's up to you!
(Almost immediately, she calms down. As Joey begins to walk through the house calling Jessica's name, he hears voices out on the deck. He slides the door open and there sits Jessica and

two of her friends drinking energy drinks and smoking cigarettes. Jessica pops up out her chair and drops her cigarette. She didn't want Joey to see her smoking. But, the smell on her breath is a dead giveaway.)

JESSICA ALLEN: Joey, what you doing here! And who are all of these people?

JOEY ALLEN: You're smoking Jessica?

JESSICA ALLEN: Joey what's going on and who are these people?

JOEY ALLEN: They're here to help me, and I'm here to help you. I'm taking you back to North Carolina to live with me! I'm gonna get full custody of you!

JESSICA ALLEN: What? Don't I have some say so in all of this?

JOEY ALLEN: What are you talking about? I thought you wanted to come live with me.

JESSICA ALLEN: At one time I did, but not anymore! I don't want to leave all of my friends and my school! You can't just bust in here with half the town and take control of my life, Joey!

JOEY ALLEN: I'm not trying to take control of your life, I'm trying to save it. I can't believe you're acting like this Jess. For years you've talked about living with me.

JESSICA ALLEN: Things are different now, Joey. I want to stay here in Tennessee, I don't want to go to North Carolina.

AGENT OSBORNE: I'm sorry Jessica, but at this point, you don't have a choice in the matter. Either you're going to North Carolina with your brother, or you're going to a foster home until this whole thing is resolved in court. We cannot, and will not, leave you here. So you need to decide and decide right now, because I'm not in the mood to play this round and round game with you. This environment you're living in, by law, is considered unsafe and unhealthy for your wellbeing. And for that reason alone, you will not remain in this home. So, what's it gonna be?
(Jessica looks at Joey with extreme anger on her face as she walks past him to go in the house to pack.)

JESSICA ALLEN: I hate you!
(Joey's heart sinks. "I hate you" is the last thing he ever thought he'd hear her say to him. But, in spite of what's happening, in his heart, he knows he's doing the right thing.)

FOURTEEN

(Back in North Carolina, Devin, who now has more money than he ever thought he'd have, is living it up. In only six months, he has doubled Mr. President's clientele, doubled the cash flow coming in, and doubled his status within the organization. Not only has he established himself as a power earner, he has also established himself as a power player. But with his newfound power, come a lot of newfound enemies. Devin and Mr. President have gotten closer over the months, and their relationship is not looked upon as a positive thing in the eyes of the other guys. So, they take it upon themselves to share their concerns in their weekly meeting with Mr. President. As the meeting is about to close, Mr. President opens the floor for comments as he always does.)

MR. PRESIDENT: Anybody have anything to say before we close?
(The guys look at each other waiting to see who's going speak up first.)

MR. PRESIDENT: Well, it's obvious that you've got something on your minds, so let's hear it.
(City, the guy that handles the money, speaks up.)

CITY: You've let your guard down brother, and that's dangerous.

MR. PRESIDENT: Since you're the first one to speak up, I assume you're talking about Devin.

CITY: That's exactly who I'm talking about.

MR. PRESIDENT: What is it this time, City? What has he done to scare you this time?
(187, the organization's killer, decides to speak up as well.)

187: See that's what we're talking about. You think we're intimidated, or jealous of Devin, but it's none of that. Money will not keep you on top of what we do. How you go about business, to make that money, is what keeps you on top of what we do. Experience is what it's all about, and that comes in time. You're giving him way too much, way too soon and he can't handle it. He's moving ahead of the game. He's starting to create his own rules, instead of following the ones already written. Devin has only been down with us for less than a year, and already you've given him access to things that we didn't even know existed, and we've been with you for almost twenty years. You don't operate that way man, you never have. You've always told us that there are certain parts of your life we will never know about. And you know what, that's cool. We've never questioned that, but what you're exposing this kid to, and the time you're spending with him, is dangerous. He can't handle it. There are certain lines that are laid out, that are never to be crossed. Devin is starting to cross those lines, and he's crossing them because he doesn't see them. You're confusing him, and giving him mixed signals with this buddy, buddy thing you guys have going on. The lines are disappearing right before his eyes, and it's going to get him, or all of us, killed.

CITY: Do you know that instead of calling me, and setting up a meeting to make a money drop, that fool showed up at my house unannounced. He knocked on my door, and handed me two suitcases of cash right there in front of my wife. Not even you would do something like that. We've made it very clear that our homes are off limits when it comes to business. But he doesn't care. He thinks that certain rules don't apply to him. And because of that, he's gonna cross the wrong line one-day, and it's gonna cost us everything.

187: If he ever shows up at my house, I'm gonna drag him off somewhere, and I'm killing him. He's as good as dead.
(Mr. President sits there, and looks at each one of the guys, then he leans forward, putting his elbows on the table.

MR. PRESIDENT: Anything else?
(The guys all look at each other in amazement. They can't believe his "I don't care attitude.")

CITY: Are you serious, man? You don't have anything at all to say?

MR. PRESIDENT: Oh no, I have something to say. But, I think I'll save it for another time. Because if I respond right now, the way I want to respond, things are not going to go well in here, you get what I'm saying? Y'all are coming apart at the seams, and I don't like it. So I'm gonna let all of you leave, while you still can. And when I'm ready to respond, I'll call you. Now get out of my office.

CITY: Talk to me, man.
(Mr. President stands up and screams at the top of his lungs!)

MR. PRESIDENT: Get out of my office before I kill you!
(An eerie silence immediately takes control of the room. As they look at Mr. President, and the rage that blankets his face, one by one they begin to stand up and walk towards the door. City is the last one out. Just before he leaves, he turns and faces Mr. President.)

CITY: I am just trying to watch out for you, man.

MR. PRESIDENT: Get out!
(City turns and slowly walks out, closing the door behind him. Mr. President sits down, and begins to question whether the men he once called loyal, have now become his most dangerous foes.)

FIFTEEN

(As Devin is standing out on his upstairs deck, he says to himself.)

DEVIN COX: If they could see me now. I'm paid, I'm in charge, and I'm the man.
(The phone rings.)

DEVIN COX: Hello.
(It's his mother's brother, his uncle Will.)

UNCLE WILL: Devin, it's your Uncle Will.

DEVIN COX: What up, Uncle Will!

UNCLE WILL: Devin, it's your mama. We had to rush her to the hospital.
(He's in complete shock.)

DEVIN COX: What!

UNCLE WILL: I went by to check on her, and found her lying in the middle of the living room floor.

DEVIN COX: Is she gonna be all right?

UNCLE WILL: Right now we're waiting to hear from the doctor. We've been here for about two hours. Can you come home?
(Devin doesn't answer. As the reality of what's happened sets in, he starts to cry. He can't say a word.)

UNCLE WILL: Are you there?
(He swallows the lump in his throat, and quietly responds.)

DEVIN COX: I'm here.

UNCLE WILL: Can you make it home son?

DEVIN COX: I'm on my way.

UNCLE WILL: Now, Devin, you make sure you get your head together before you get on the road. I don't want you to end up in the hospital too.

DEVIN COX: I'm good, Uncle Will.

UNCLE WILL: Okay. Well, I guess I'll see you in a few hours.

DEVIN COX: Uncle Will, if anything happens before I get there, you make sure you tell mama I love her.

UNCLE WILL: She's gonna be all right. Your mama is in the hands of Jesus. She'll be just fine, just pray for her.

DEVIN COX: I'm gonna get packed, I'll see you soon.

(Devin hangs up the phone, falls to his knees, and cries. Not only is he scared for his mother, he's also dealing with the guilt of all of this possibly being his fault. He knew his mother was fasting, and not eating because of everything that was going on with him. The bible says, "Some things come only through fasting and praying." Mama Lucy was determined to find out what was going on with her baby. He felt so alone, and he just needed a friend, but he's alienated the two closest friends he had. He never returns their phone calls. He rarely texted them back when they texted him. Mr. President doesn't allow any of his guys to use social media. The scripture says, "After pride comes a fall." God uses our parents and others to warn us of trouble. When we ignore those warnings, often times God will hand us over to ourselves. Time has always proven that we are our own worst enemy. Devin's prideful fall is a hard one, and it's a hard one that's just beginning. His parents have always taught him to call on the name of Jesus, but his ego and his out of control lifestyle have consumed him so much to the point that he doesn't even remember that it is that very name that can provide his way of escape.)

SIXTEEN

(As Jessica continues to settle into her new life with Joey, things seem to go from bad to worse. As much as Joey tries, he just can't seem to cheer her up, or at times, calm her down. The emotional scars that have been left from the sexual abuse, have really taken its toll on her. But, in spite of all of fighting, Joey has managed to find a little sunshine in the midst of all of the rain. Joey is going to ask Jenna to marry him. They've been together since they were eighteen years old, and neither one of them have ever been happier. With both of them being State grads, Joey still has some alumni connections. He calls the associate director of the drama department, and reserves the campus auditorium. He had his friend set up a table in the center of the big beautiful stage. The stage is completely surrounded with rose scented candles, that's Jenna's favorite flower. The table is gorgeously decorated with candles, flowers, creased linen napkins, antique china, and sterling silver utensils. It's Jenna's birthday, and Joey told her that he has a surprise for her. For the entire ride over to the campus Jenna has been wearing a blind fold. Once they arrive, he parks the car in front of the auditorium and carefully walks her up the stairs. As they approach the doors to the auditorium, Jenna gets a whiff of the rose scented candles.)

JENNA WOODS: Nice, I smell roses.

JOEY ALLEN: Yes, you do. Now I want you to be careful, don't take too big of a step.
(Joey guides her down the somewhat steep steps leading to the stage. After walking onto the stage, sitting her down, Joey walks around and sits in his chair.)

JOEY ALLEN: Okay, you can take off your blind fold.
(Jenna slowly removes the blind fold. She can't believe her eyes. She looks around and can't believe what he's done.)

JENNA WOODS: Joey, are you kidding me? I can't believe this, you did all of this for me?

JOEY ALLEN: I would do anything for you.
(Jenna can't stop smiling as she looks around and takes it all in.)

JENNA WOODS: How did you do this?

JOEY ALLEN: Very carefully.

JENNA WOODS: All of this for me, I just can't believe it.
(Joey gets up, walks over to her, and gets down on one knee.)

JOEY WOODS: You know that job I applied for with that software company that makes all of the software for college vet schools? They called me last week. They offered me a position and I took it.
(Jenna gives him a huge hug.)

JENNA WOODS: Oh, Joey, I'm so happy for you! Congratulations, baby!

JOEY ALLEN: Don't be happy for me.
(Joey pulls out the ring box and opens it.)

JOEY ALLEN: Be happy for us.
(Jenna covers her mouth with her hands as her eyes fill with happy tears. And not long after her tears start to fall, Joey begins to cry.)

JOEY ALLEN: I got the job I wanted, and now I want the girl I need. Jenna, you have changed my life in ways you can't even imagine. Good or bad, you've held on. You believed in me in times when I didn't believe in myself. You helped me through all of the drama with my family, and most of all, you have loved me like I've never been loved before. I love you, I need you, I admire you, and I want to know, if you'll make my life complete, by being my wife. Jenna, will you marry me?
(She's so overcome by her emotions that she can't even respond. She eventually gathers enough strength to answer.)

JENNA WOODS: Joey, I would love, and be honored to marry you.
(As they hold each other tight, with their young hearts content with a future together, the darkness in the auditorium slowly disappears.)

JENNA WOODS: What's going on?

JOEY ALLEN: Another little surprise I have for you. Look out there.
(Jenna looks to her left towards the auditorium seats, and to her surprise, sitting on the seventh row, are her parents. Joey asks them to drive into town to be a part of the proposal. Again, she begins to cry.)

JENNA WOODS: Mom, Dad!
(Her parents walk up onto the stage and the three of them hold each other tight as they all shed tears of joy.)

SEVENTEEN

(It's now 6:30 in the morning in North Carolina, and Devin is just arriving at the hospital. He stops at the nurse's desk just down the hall from his mom's room and asks to speak with her doctor. Mama Lucy's doctor is the same doctor she's had for many years, so Devin knows he's going to get the honest truth about what's going on with her. Dr. Shari Smith is making her rounds, so they have to page her. In a matter of a minute, Dr. Smith arrives at the desk.)

DR. SMITH: Devin, how are you?
(Because they've known each other for ten plus years, they're practically like family. They greet each other with a hug as they always do.)

DEVIN COX: I've been better. What's going on with mama? Or better yet let me guess, all of that fasting she's been doing made her sick?

DR. SMITH: Well, Devin, she's got a nasty lump on her head. She said she looked up to change a light bulb, and that's all she remembers. We've run some tests, and we think it may be vertigo, we're not sure yet. Dizziness is associated with it and people who suffer from it experience the effect of things around them spinning or moving. We think she may have had an episode, and it caused her to fall and hit her head. Looking up can often times trigger this spinning effect.

DEVIN COX: So, what happens next?

DR. SMITH: We'll wait for her test results and go from there. (Dr. Smith can see that Devin is worried. Mama Lucy is all he has.)

DR. SMITH: She's gonna be all right, Devin.

DEVIN COX: Can I go in and see her?

DR. SMITH: She's sleeping right now, and she really needs to get some rest. But, I tell you what, I'll get you a couple of blankets, and you can sleep on the pull out couch. When she wakes up in the morning, your face will be the first thing she sees. And, I'm sure that will make her day.

DEVIN COX: Okay.
(After getting settled in, Devin is fast asleep. Between the long drive, and the stress, he's worn out. After five hours of very peaceful sleep, a gentle hand grabs Devin's shoulder and slowly moves him back and forth.)

LUCY COX: Baby.
(Devin slowly opens his eyes and sees his mother smiling at him.)

DEVIN COX: Mama?
(He immediately jumps up and hugs her.)

LUCY COX: How are you, baby?

DEVIN COX: Mama, I'm so glad you're okay. I was scared.

LUCY COX: There's nothing to be scared about, baby. God's not through with me yet.

DEVIN COX: Let me help you over to your bed.

LUCY COX: I don't need any help, Devin. I can get around on my own.
(She gingerly makes her way back to her bed with Devin trailing close behind. After making herself comfortable, Devin sits down on the bed and gently grabs her hand.)

DEVIN COX: How are you feeling mama?

LUCY COX: I'm a little tired, but I'm all right.

DEVIN COX: Mama, we've got to figure out what's going on with you. I don't want anything to happen to you.

LUCY COX: Enough about me, let's talk about you.
(Devin takes a deep breath.)

LUCY COX: How are you doing up there in Raleigh?

DEVIN COX: I'm doing really good, mama, I really am.

LUCY COX: Are you in any trouble, Devin? Now, before you answer that, you think about that question. And, don't you lie to me.

DEVIN COX: No mama, I'm not in trouble mama.
(She stares at him as if she were looking into his soul. She knows he's lying to her.)

DEVIN COX: I have a good job, I'm making good money, and things are going pretty well.

LUCY COX: Devin, I'm too old, and too tied to Jesus to sit around and worry about you. I know you, and I know when something's bothering you. That's one of the many blessings that come out of fasting. God brings clarity to the things going on around you. He keeps confusion away, long enough for you to see what's going on. I'm done, Devin. I'm gonna leave you in the hands of Jesus. I don't know exactly what's going on with you up there in Raleigh, but I do know that whatever it is, only God can get you out of it.
(Devin looks down at the floor as the shame wraps itself around his heart. He can see the disappointment on his mother's face, and that hurts him more than anything. All he's ever wanted to do is make her proud.)

DEVIN COX: Mama…
(She cuts him off in mid-sentence.)

LUCY COX: No. We're not gonna talk about it. You can't seem to get the truth to rise to the surface. So us talking about it is pointless. Now come here.

(She opens her arms to hug him.)

LUCY COX: Your father and I have always told you, that no matter what you do with your life, we'll always love you. I love you, son, and you know I do. Jesus is all you have, Devin. When the time comes, and you need Him, just call Him. Trust me, He will hear you.
(As he holds his mother, he faces the reality that the world he now lives in, is a world he can never escape from. The fear that comes with that world has convinced him that the grave is his only way of escape, not Jesus. As Mama Lucy continues to hold her son, he gets a text from Joey and Jenna. He walks over to the nightstand beside the pull-out he slept on and grabs his phone.)

DEVIN COX: Oh, my goodness!

LUCY COX: What is it?

DEVIN COX: Joey and Jenna got engaged yesterday.

LUCY COX: Well, praise the Lord!

DEVIN COX: He wants me to be his best man.
(Lucy notices a strange look on his face.)

LUCY COX: You seem surprised.

DEVIN COX: No, I'm not surprised, I miss our time together.

LUCY COX: You don't hang out anymore?

DEVIN COX: Everybody got busy with life all of a sudden. N.C. State decided to keep Jenna on as an employee after she graduated. With her being an instructor now she works quite a bit. And Joey, last I heard, was waiting tables somewhere in Raleigh. He was working Monday through Saturday. Sometimes doing double shifts.
(Devin gave every reason, except the real reason, as to why they don't hangout anymore.)

LUCY COX: I've always loved those two like they were my own. You all need to make time for each other, Devin.

DEVIN COX: Yeah, I know mama.
(Disappointed by the fact that the relationships he once had with Joey, and Jenna will never be what they once were, Devin begins the all too familiar grappling process with his two new friends: Shame and Guilt. A month or so later, Joey is back in Tennessee in court fighting for the custody of his sister, Jessica. Things are still a little rough at home between the two of them, but it's getting better. Having Jenna around gives Jessica an outlet to vent, and talk about how she feels. The custody battle has gotten so ugly, that Joey and his parents don't even bother to look at each other. After witness testimonies, and the lawyers going back and forth, the judge has granted Joey temporary legal custody over Jessica. C.P.S. agent Sara Osborne's testimony, is the one that convinced the judge that she's better off with Joey. After dismissal, Joey's lawyer pulls him to the side and gives him some amazing news.)

JOEY'S LAWYER: I received a call from Paul Miller's lawyer. He entered a plea of guilty on all charges. He admitted to everything he ever did to Jessica, in exchange for a lighter sentence.

JOEY ALLEN: How much lighter?

JOEY'S LAWYER: Their offering 25 years, instead of 40. Now we can accept the plea and move on. Or, we can fight it and go for the whole thing.

JOEY ALLEN: What do you think?

JOEY'S LAWYER: To be honest with you, I think we should accept the plea. I say that for Jessica's sake. If we fight this thing, she will have to get on the stand and face him again, and probably more than once. You said yourself that she's come a long way. Throwing her back into something like this could set her back for years. Think about it, you'll be asking her to relive it all over again.
(Joey looks over at Jessica.)

JOEY ALLEN: Let's take the deal. It's time to move on.

JOEY'S LAWYER: I will call him first thing in the morning.
(As Joey's mom and dad leave the courtroom, Joey's mom, Betty Allen, tries to talk to Jessica. Joey hurries across the room to interrupt what he sees as possible trouble.)

JOEY ALLEN: Don't you say one word to her!

JESSICA ALLEN: Joey stop it!

BETTY ALLEN: She is still our daughter!

JOEY ALLEN: You gave up that right the day you handed her over to your drinking and your pedophile friends.

JESSICA ALLEN: I'm over it! I am over it, and I'm over all of you!
(Jessica takes off running out of the courtroom.)

JENNA WOODS: Can't you guys just give her a break?
(Jenna goes after her.)

EIGHTEEN

(As the months have gone by, Devin, Joey, and Jenna have been a little bit better about keeping in touch with each other. They've decided to get together to celebrate the engagement. The plan is to meet at Joey's place. That was Devin's suggestion for two reasons. One, he didn't want to be caught with Joey and Jenna in his house by any of the members of Congress. And two, he wanted to see Joey's sister, Jessica. The big night of celebration has arrived, and Devin is standing at Joey's door about to ring the doorbell. Instead, he starts to drum on the door as he sings.)

JOEY ALLEN: I know who that is!
(Joey is so excited to see his friend. It's been a little over a year since they've seen each other. Joey stands close to the door.)

JOEY ALLEN: If you're trying to serenade me it's too late, I'm taken.

DEVIN COX: Please, baby! Please!
(Joey opens the door and immediately Devin tries to hug him.)

JOEY ALLEN: Freeze!

(Joey puts his hand on Devin's chest and stops him.)

JOEY ALLEN: Some things never change my friend!

DEVIN COX: Joey it's been over a year man! You can't give me a hug?

JOEY ALLEN: Like 1 said, some things never change.

DEVIN COX: You're a trip dude!
(Devin finally accepts that a handshake is all he's going to get. Joey closes the door, and Devin begins to look around Joey's place.)

DEVIN COX: Is Jenna living here?

JOEY ALLEN: Are you crazy? No, she doesn't live here.

DEVIN COX: Well, 1 know you didn't decorate this place.

JOEY ALLEN: As a matter of fact 1 did.

DEVIN COX: With Jenna's help.

JOEY ALLEN: Nope. It was all me.

DEVIN COX: 1'm impressed. No beer lights, and no posters. 1 am really impressed.
(Jessica walks into the living room.)

DEVIN COX: There she is! There's my little sis!

(Devin gives her a big hug.)

DEVIN COX: Look at you! You're as tall as I am.

JESSICA ALLEN: That's not saying a whole lot, Devin.

DEVIN COX: You a comedian now, huh?

JESSICA COX: I'm just kidding.

DEVIN COX: How are you doing?

JOEY ALLEN: She's doing awesome. She made the softball team, she's gonna be the starting pitcher.

JESSICA ALLEN: We don't know that quite yet.

JOEY ALLEN: She smoked those girls in tryouts, you should have seen her!

DEVIN COX: That's my girl!
(There's a knock on the door.)

JOEY ALLEN: Come in!
(It's Jenna.)

JENNA WOODS: Well, well, well. Who is this stranger?
(Devin smiles at Jenna, but his smile isn't what it seems. No longer is Jenna the cool childhood best friend he's always known. Now, she's the beautiful adult woman he's never seen. Although he's able to hide it, in his mind, he not only sees a

different Jenna, he sees a Jenna he thinks he may want. Devin's reality is so distorted, that he only cares about what Devin wants. That spirit of greed, control, and manipulation has become the foundation of his logic. There are no boundary lines in his life, just the mindset of entitlement and arrogance. If he can't have what he wants, then why not just take it. That's his new way of rationalizing things.)

JENNA WOODS: Are you gonna stand there like a zombie? Or, are you gonna give me a hug?
(He's absolutely mesmerized by how beautiful she is. He's also more than happy to give her a hug. After the hug, he steps back and takes a look at her.)

DEVIN COX: I think I'm gonna take her from you, Joe.
(That comment creates a somewhat awkward feeling in the room because Devin has always treated Jenna like his little sister. The comment has somewhat crossed the line. But Devin, with his new slick hustler's mentality, smooths the whole thing over.

DEVIN COX: They say that married couples begin to look alike after a few years of marriage. So, I think I'll take her from you to save her from that face of yours. Look at that face, Jenna.
 (Devin turns her towards Joey.)

DEVIN COX: Do you really want to end up with a face like that?

JENNA WOODS: Awe, I love this face, and I don't mind looking like this face either.

(Jenna walks over to Joey and gives him a kiss. Devin doesn't show it, but watching her kiss Joey bothered him. It created somewhat of a feeling of resentment towards Joey. But in typical Devin fashion, he files it away to deal with another time. Later on that night while the three of them are sitting at the table in the bar, Joey surprises Jenna with some awesome news.)

JOEY ALLEN: Honey, guess what.

JENNA WOODS: What?

JOEY ALLEN: They offered me a new position at work, I got a promotion.
(Jenna's face lights up.)

JENNA WOODS: Are you serious? What's the position?

JOEY ALLEN: Assistant Supervisor over manufacturing.
(Jenna leans over and gives him a hug. Devin grabs his drink and turns his head looking in another direction. He's completely over all of the affection between the two of them. He sees the love they have for each other, and it bothers him because he desires the same thing. But, he doesn't want his own love, he wants Joey's love. He wants Jenna.)

JENNA WOODS: Are you gonna take it?

JOEY ALLEN: It depends. If I take it, I'll have to work the eleven to seven shift. Which might work out just fine. I could get off work, take Jess to school, go home, sleep, and then pick her up from school. And when she starts softball, I won't have to rush home to get her to practice.

JENNA WOODS: But, you can't leave her at home by herself all night.

JOEY ALLEN: I know. I was wondering if you could stay at my place at night with her.

JENNA WOODS: I guess I could. You know what, that would be fun. I'd love to.

JOEY ALLEN: Cool. We have a meeting in the morning and I will let them know that I want the position.
(It seems like everything is falling right in line for Joey and Jenna. They are so excited about starting this new chapter of their lives. But it's a chapter that will not be written without Devin, not if he can help it.)

NINETEEN

(It's now a year and a half later. Joey and Jenna are newlyweds. Jessica is doing great, and making progress every day. Life is really good. Joey and Jenna had an amazingly beautiful wedding, but it was a wedding that did not include Joey's parents. He didn't invite either one of them. The last thing he wanted was for them to show up drunk and ruin their special day. When they went back to court for the custody hearing, his dad showed up reeking of alcohol. The smell was so strong, that the judge thought it might be best if they reschedule, but his drinking is what made it obvious to the court that Jessica needed to stay with Joey for good. The judge granted Joey and Jenna full custody. Joey's mom didn't even show up for the hearing. Joey had heard that his parents had split up and were possibly getting a divorce. Their drinking was killing every part of their lives. Joey was rapidly moving up the ladder at work. He had since been promoted twice, and was now the overall site supervisor for the entire division. Although he was still working third shift, he and Jenna have managed to create a system that works very well for their family. It's now the month of January, and Devin's birthday is one week away. Both Joey and Jenna are planning to go to the party Devin is having. But at the last minute, literally three minutes before they're going to walk out of the door, Joey gets a call. There's a problem with the systems program at work. They need him right away.)

JOEY ALLEN: Honey, I can't go to the party.

JENNA ALLEN: Are you serious?

JOEY ALLEN: The program at work shut down and I have to get it up and running. We can't have that thing down all night. It could cost us hundreds of thousands of dollars. But, you can still go without me.

JENNA ALLEN: But, he's expecting both of us.

JOEY ALLEN: I can't go Jenna. I told you when I took this position that this type of thing could happen. I'm sorry honey. But, I still want you to go.
(Jenna contemplates whether she should go by herself or not.)

JENNA ALLEN: I'll give Devin a call and let him know that we won't be able to make it. I think I'm just gonna stay home and watch a movie.

JOEY ALLEN: Are you sure?

JENNA ALLEN: Yeah. I'm gonna get in my pajamas and then I'll call him.

JOEY ALLEN: All right. Tell him I'm sorry and I'll catch up with him later.

(Joey gives Jenna a hug, a kiss, an 'I love you' and heads out the door. Jenna changes into her pajamas and sits down on the couch. She calls Devin to let him know that they are not coming. When she calls, Devin sees her name on his caller ID.)

DEVIN COX: What's up Jenna? You guys on your way?

JENNA ALLEN: Devin we're not gonna make it, I'm really sorry.

DEVIN COX: Come on Jenna, are you serious?

JENNA ALLEN: I'm really sorry, Devin. They called Joey into work at the last minute, and I really don't want to go by myself.

DEVIN COX: You won't be by yourself, I'll be here! Jenna, I was looking forward to you guys being here tonight. I miss my best friends. We can hardly ever find time to get together anymore. Please come to my party and celebrate my birthday with me please, you're my best friend. You won't even have to drive, I'll send you a car.

JENNA ALLEN: What do you mean?

DEVIN COX: My boss has a limo business on the side, and he told me I could use it tonight for my guests if I needed it. (Again, Jenna contemplates on going or not.)

JENNA ALLEN: Okay. I'll come for a little while, but I'm not staying very long.

DEVIN COX: Fair enough. Do you want me to send the car?

JENNA ALLEN: Sure why not. How often do you get a free limo?

DEVIN COX: I'll have him at your door in thirty minutes.

JENNA ALLEN: I'll see you soon.
(They hang up the phone. Immediately, Devin's mind goes into scam mode. He looks at this as the opportunity of a lifetime. This is the window he's been waiting for. He'll have Jenna in his environment, on his terms, alone, and without Joey. He's planning on taking full advantage of Joey's absence. As soon as Jenna walks in the door, Devin is on. He introduces her to all of his friends, and every introduction is stapled to a compliment. After smooth talking, and convincing Jenna to have more drinks, Devin realizes that keeping her at the party is now just a matter of amping up the fun. So he tells the D.J. to kick up the music. Right away, that takes the party to a whole new level.

DEVIN COX: I know it's probably been a long time since you've danced, but I'll go out there and let you embarrass me anyway. Let's go.
(Without hesitation, Jenna jumps up and heads for the dance floor. They spend the next thirty minutes on the dance floor going wild. The D.J. decides to slow things down, by playing a much slower romantic song.)

DEVIN COX: You're a married woman, so I think we should skip out on this one!

JENNA ALLEN: I agree!
(That suggestion made Devin look like a true gentleman. But the devil's tricks are always calm, before they become catastrophic. They walk over to the fully stocked bar Devin has in his basement and order a drink.)

DEVIN COX: Would you like to see the rest of the house?

JENNA ALLEN: This is your house?

DEVIN COX: Yes mam.

JENNA ALLEN: What do you do, Devin? We have no idea what you do.

DEVIN COX: I'm the North Carolina Regional Director for a Pharmaceutical company.

JENNA ALLEN: What about your music? Did you just lose your love for it? I thought that's what you wanted to do.

DEVIN COX: I'll always love music. I just decided to go in another direction.

JENNA ALLEN: As long as you're happy I guess.
(They are now standing on the balcony alone.)

JENNA ALLEN: So when are you gonna settle down, Devin? You can't live the party life forever.

DEVIN COX: I don't live the party life. Don't get me wrong, I still like to go out and have a good time every now and then. But, I work a lot, I don't have time to live the party life. Let me ask you something. Have you ever tried this?
(He pulls a very small plastic bag with a little cocaine in it out of his pocket.)

JENNA ALLEN: Is that what I think it is?

DEVIN COX: It's cocaine.

JENNA ALLEN: Devin, what are you doing with that stuff?

DEVIN COX: A buddy of mine gave it to me for my birthday. I've never tried it, but I want to.

JENNA ALLEN: Well, you go ahead. I'll pass.
(Devin carefully opens the bag, sticks a key inside, puts some on the key, and snorts it. He looks at Jenna, takes a deep breath, and slowly shakes his head in disbelief. It gives him an immediate high.)

DEVIN COX: Wow! Oh my goodness! You have got to try it!

JENNA ALLEN: How does it feel?

DEVIN COX: You have got to try it!
(With her judgment somewhat impaired because of the amount of alcohol that she's had, the temptation to do cocaine quickly turns into turmoil. She knows it's wrong, she knows she shouldn't do it, and she knows deep down in her heart

that it will be the single biggest mistake of her life. Devin has always had the gift of influence. His mother always said that her son could sell a bank money. So when he saw Jenna struggling with her decision, he took it upon himself to help her make it.)

DEVIN COX: Come on Jen. Just this one time and I'll flush the rest. We'll do a little bit and that's it. It's a one-time deal, let's just go for it! And think about it, you're not even driving tonight. It's my birthday, homegirl. Let's enjoy it! We've all done well for ourselves, we're successful, and life is great, Jenna. (After a long pause, Jenna responds.)

JENNA ALLEN: Okay, just this one time. And after this, you'll flush the rest, deal?

DEVIN COX: Deal.
(Devin dips the key in, puts it up to her nose, and Jenna takes the first step on the road that is going to absolutely derail the rest of her life. Her marriage, her parents, her job, her relationship with Jessica, and her self-respect, will all eventually have to take the mighty blow that cocaine promises. It's a blow that's hard, it's destructive, it doesn't discriminate, and it doesn't care about titles. It's patient, it tortures, and it doesn't give its victims back. She is now experiencing the beginning of the end.)

DEVIN COX: Okay. That's our one time, I'm gonna flush the rest.
(Devin turns to go to the bathroom to flush the rest.)

JENNA ALLEN: Let's try a little more.
(The demon of addiction has found a new home.)

DEVIN COX: But, you said just one time.

JENNA ALLEN: I meant after we finish what you have there. After this one little bag is what I meant.
(Devin knew she was lying. He also knew that his plan worked. He was hoping that what he had seen happen to many other people the first time they tried cocaine, would happen to Jenna, and it did. If things go the way he thinks they're going to go, she'll be calling, meeting with, and spending a lot more time with him, which ultimately will end in the shedding of innocent blood. As Jenna parties the night away, Joey is at work trying to fix the computer program problem. As he searches through the system, in walks a man named Patrick Kerry.)

PATRICK KERRY: Joey?
(Joey spins his chair around.)

JOEY ALLEN: Yes.

PATRICK KERRY: I'm Patrick Kerry.
(They shake hands.)

PARTICK KERRY: I'm the new in-house tech.

JOEY ALLEN: They said they were going to get me some help, I guess they finally did it. Welcome aboard.

PATRICK KERRY: Thanks. What can I help you with?

(The two of them hit it off immediately. Not only do they work well together, they have a lot in common, and that's how Jesus works. Jesus said, "I will supply all of your needs," and Joey is going to need a lot. Everything is about timing when it comes to God, everything. Patrick walking into Joey's life is no accident, and it's not a coincidence. Patrick is a forty-eight year old white Christian man that God has sent to help Joey survive the journey that Jenna has decided to take the two of them on. A journey that will be taken by them, but navigated by Devin. As the months go by, Jenna's cocaine use changes from once every couple of months, to twice every month. When Joey goes to work at night, and Jessica goes to bed, Jenna digs deep into the back of her closet and pulls out her stash of cocaine. The once loving, straight A, vibrant, athletic young lady, has taken a path where no human should ever go. When she runs out of drugs, she calls Devin who is more than happy to supply her. Every now and then he gives her drugs for free, because he knows that it will keep her coming back. Like most addicts, Jenna has been able to hide her drug use. She goes to work, she keeps the house clean, and she maintains what everybody around her knows to be normal. A year later, just when her drug use is about to reach a whole new level, Jenna gets pregnant. She thought that maybe it was the cocaine that was making her sick in the morning. But it wasn't the drugs, it was the blessing from God that some couples never have the opportunity to experience, it was the gift of life. Joey was over the moon about being a father. He not only sees this as a chance to redeem what he missed out on with his own father, he sees this as another opportunity to get ever closer to what some may call the most fantastic wife in the world. With most women, news of a baby is news that brings them a joy they can't explain. But with Jenna, it brings her to a crossroad she can't understand. In the reality of what's at stake, it should be a no brainer. But in the addict's mind, there is no reality, just the next high. That's where she comes face to face with the depth of her addiction for the very first time. In spite of the beautiful life she's carrying, she can't ignore the craving for cocaine her body is calling for. For days on end, she struggles with her addiction. She's not herself, she's unusually impatient, she's very short tempered, and her body is starting to make her feel like she's losing all control. Although Joey and Jessica are dealing with the wrath of her addiction, they extend her grace and tie it all to pregnancy hormones. One night while Joey is at work, and Jessica is out at a sleep over, Jenna is left all alone with her cravings, the voice of the demon of addiction, and her unborn baby. As she paces the floor, and begins to sweat from minor withdrawals, Jenna sits down on the couch and begins to cry. She thinks back to the night she tried cocaine for the first time with Devin, and desperately wishes she could do it all over again. Like lots of addicts, Jenna has reached the point of acceptance. The addiction's voice has convinced her that she will always be an addict, and that getting clean is not only impossible, it's a secret that she can't tell anybody about. She thinks about how disappointed her parents would be. She thinks about how disappointed Joey would be. She thinks about the shame and guilt of people knowing she's addicted to drugs. She decides to keep it all inside, and not talk to anybody. That decision is what takes her over the edge into deep depression. To avoid the pain that comes with the reality of what she's done, Jenna does what all addicts do, she chooses to experience the illusion of escape from her problems by getting high. Not even the sweet life she's carrying can create a moment of pause. She calls Devin to see if he will give her some drugs. She doesn't know that he's a drug dealer, she just thinks that he has easy access to it.)

DEVIN COX: What's up Jen?

JENNA ALLEN: What are you up to?

DEVIN COX: Just hanging out at home watching the game.

JENNA ALLEN: You wouldn't happen to have a little treat on you would you?

DEVIN COX: You're not getting addicted to that stuff are you? (Devin is playing the game of deception with perfection. He knows she's got a problem, and he's about to take full advantage of it.)

JENNA ALLEN: Are you crazy? No, I'm not getting addicted, come on, this is Jenna you're talking to.

DEVIN COX: I was just looking out for you.

JENNA ALLEN: I'm fine.

DEVIN COX: I don't have any on me right now, but I can get it. How much do you want?

JENNA ALLEN: Well, that was my next question. Can you look out for me one more time? I don't have the money right now. (That's exactly what Devin wanted to hear.)

DEVIN COX: I'll take care of you. Come on over.
(With Jenna so early in her pregnancy, Devin can't possibly tell she's pregnant. Once she arrives at his place, she comes in and sits down on the couch. Devin pulls out a small tray, with a very small amount of cocaine on it. Jenna hesitantly picks up the straw. As she's sitting there staring at the drugs, Devin can tell that something is bothering her.)

DEVIN COX: Is there something wrong?
(Jenna realizes the magnitude of what she is about to do. But the addiction could care less. She leans forward, hovers slightly above the cocaine, and sniffs. Not only does she get the high she was looking for, she gets her unborn baby high on cocaine for the first time. After a few more sniffs, the drugs are all gone.)

JENNA ALLEN: Is that all you have?

DEVIN COX: I've got a little more.

JENNA COX: Can I have a little?

DEVIN COX: What about me?

JENNA ALLEN: We can both do some.

DEVIN COX: That's not what I'm talking about. What's in it for me?

JENNA ALLEN: I'll pay you back, I promise.

DEVIN COX: I don't want your money. I want you.
(Jenna absolutely cannot believe what she's hearing.)

JENNA COX: I'm married, and you're my husband's best friend! Why would say something like that?

DEVIN COX: We're not kids anymore Jenna. I don't know who Joey is anymore. We never talk, we don't hang out, and to be honest with you, I've moved on. I've got a different life, with different people, and this is a different time. You can always get up and leave, Jenna. I'm not holding you here against your will.
(She can't believe who, and what Devin has become. Without saying a word, she gets up and heads for the door.)

DEVIN COX: If you leave, you will not come back! I won't even take your phone calls! If you want to get high, you'll get it yourself!
(That stops Jenna in her tracks. She turns around to face Devin. After they stand there staring at each other for a few seconds, Devin walks over to his bedroom, and opens the door never saying a word. With every bit of shame a human can carry in their heart, Jenna makes her way across the floor into Devin's bedroom, taking with her, her baby, her vows, her marriage, and the last little bit of dignity she had left. She takes all of those precious things, and places them at the doorstep of what is soon to be a living hell. Jenna's addiction convinces her to throw her family away, along with all that is important in her life. Month after month, Jenna continues to spiral out of control, taking her unborn baby along for the ride. By month seven, it's obvious to Joey that something is terribly wrong.

He's never had any kind of real experience with drug addiction, just the recreational use by some of the kids in high school. While he's sitting on the couch watching a game, a sports magazine is advertising one full year's subscription, for only six months of payments. Thinking to himself that it's a good deal, Joey looks around for a pen to write down the 1-800, number. After frantically searching, he decides to look in Jenna's purse for a pen. After he digs around for a few seconds, he finds a pen. As he pulls his hand out of her purse, he notices some white powder on the tip of his finger. Joey walks over to the kitchen table, turns the light on, and dumps everything out of Jenna's purse on to the table. The sound of makeup compacts, a bottle of lotion, and keys hitting the table wakes Jenna. Because of her late night running around getting high, when she finally does sleep, she sleeps sometimes 8 or 9 hours a day. Not to mention being pregnant and how that wears her out. When Jenna walks into the kitchen, Joey is holding a small plastic bag with cocaine in it. The cocaine is slowly spilling out of the bag because of the hole Joey accidentally put in when he was looking for a pen. Just like a true addict, Jenna is more concerned about wasting cocaine, than she is about Joey's eye's filling up with tears.)

JENNA ALLEN: Joey, what are you doing!
(She hurries over to the table and carefully takes the plastic bag out of his hand as she yells at him.)

JENNA ALLEN: Who do you think you are going through my purse?

JOEY ALLEN: Jenna, are you doing cocaine?

JENNA ALLEN: I can't believe you went through my stuff!
(Jenna is now standing at the counter pouring her cocaine into another plastic bag. Joey pushes the chair in front of him over and kicks it out of his way as he makes his way over to Jenna.)

JOEY ALLEN: You're pregnant, I find cocaine, and all you care about is your stupid purse!

JENNA ALLEN: Joey, give me a break will you!

JOEY ALLEN: Are you kidding me right now? Give you a break, I'll give you a break all right!
(Joey snatches the cocaine out of her hand and heads for the bathroom. As he's walking down the hall, Jenna is screaming and pulling his shirt trying to stop him.)

JOEY ALLEN: I can't believe you would do this to our baby!
(Joey walks into the bathroom, lifts the toilet lid, and drops the whole bag in and flushes it. When he turns around to face her, she slaps him on the face and walks out. As she makes her way down the hall towards their bedroom, Joey follows her.)

JOEY ALLEN: How long have you been doing drugs Jenna?
(She ignores him. So he gets in front of her and grabs her arms to stop her.)

JOEY ALLEN: Stop and talk to me Jenna!
(She pushes him away and walks into the bedroom. Jenna puts her shoes on, grabs her long coat, and walks toward the door to leave. Joey steps in front of her, shuts the door, and locks it.)

JOEY ALLEN: Where do you think you're going? You're not leaving this house!

JENNA ALLEN: Joey, get out of my way!

JOEY ALLEN: You're gonna have to go through me to leave. Now talk to me and answer my question! How long have you been doing cocaine?
(Jenna realizes that there is no way he's going to let her leave. So she sits on the bed.)

JENNA ALLEN: Off and on for a few months okay, you happy now? Now, may I please leave?

JOEY ALLEN: Jenna, you're carrying a baby! You are carrying our child! You're turning our baby into a drug addict!
(Joey starts to cry. Not wanting to deal with the guilt of hurting him so deep, Jenna turns away from him. She doesn't want to see him cry. But turning away is not enough, and not long after, Jenna begins to cry. As she looks at the wall, and her tears hit the bed, she hears Joey sliding down the door into fetal positions on the floor. He is absolutely devastated. Jenna sits down on the floor next to him.)

JENNA ALLEN: I need help, Joey. What have I done?
(Jenna leans over on Joey as he continues to cry. He's so upset that he can't even talk.)

JENNA ALLEN: Baby, I'm so sorry. Please help me. Please help me.

(As they sit next to each other crying their hearts out, Joey turns to face her.)

JOEY ALLEN: Do you realize that our child will probably be born addicted to cocaine?
(Although she knew that was a possibility, hearing it from Joey rips her heart apart.)

JOEY ALLEN: What are we gonna do?

JENNA ALLEN: I've got to get some help.
(Joey wraps his arms around her.)

JOEY ALLEN: Tomorrow we'll got to the doctor, we'll tell him everything that's happened, and we'll go from there. But Jenna, you have to stop. You have to. I'm not going to live like this, and neither is our child.

JENNA ALLEN: I promise you on our love that I'm done.
(With a little doubt in his heart, Joey looks down at the floor.)

JENNA ALLEN: Look at me!
(He looks at her.)

JENNA ALLEN: I'm done, baby.
(He hugs her as the uncertainty of their family's future lies before him with no clarity. The bible says, "The mouth of fools are their ruin; they trap themselves with their lips." And that's exactly what has happened to Devin. As hell is breaking loose at Joey and Jenna's, hell has decided to pay Devin a visit as well. The trap he set for Jenna, now has two sets of hands in

it. With a cold beverage in his hand, Devin is sitting on his deck with his feet up, doing lines of cocaine. If there's one thing Mr. President hates, and absolutely says is off limits, is sampling the product. He made it very clear that his guys are not allowed to do drugs of any kind. As he leans over and takes another hit, his phone rings. And what do you know, it's Mr. President. Devin quickly sits up, gathers himself, and answers the phone.)

DEVIN COX: Hello.

MR. PRESIDENT: I need you to meet me at my office tomorrow afternoon at 5:00.

DEVIN COX: No problem. Is everything okay?

MR. PRESIDENT: Yeah, I need you to do a little job for me.

DEVIN COX: Yes, sir.

MR. PRESIDENT: What are you up to tonight?

DEVIN COX: Living this wonderful life you've given me. I'm out on my deck, having a cold one, just taking it all in.

MR. PRESIDENT: Well you've certainly earned it. I'll see you tomorrow.

DEVIN COX: You got it.
(Devin hangs up, and once again, his slick hustler mentality has won out. But what he doesn't know, is that the little job

Mr. President has for him, is a job that no silver tongue can get out of or around. Tomorrow, loyalty will have to be proven, not just talked about. The next day, Joey and Jenna are waiting in the doctor's office for the results of the ultra sound. The wait is almost too much to bear. The doctor comes in, sits down, and opens their file.)

DR. TILL: Well, we checked everything out, and the baby is showing signs of addiction. We're seeing a consistent irregular heartbeat, which could mean that there's been some heart damage. Were also seeing some erratic jerking motions from time to time. And that could be possible nerve damage. The baby has lost some weight, and after doing your blood work, you tested positive for cocaine.
(They both begin to cry.)

DR. TILL: Now, we have seen children born with addictions. And over the years, they get better and go on to have a good quality of life. So don't just assume the worst.
(The doctor's words fall on deaf ears. But what he has to say next does not.)

DR. TILL: There's one other thing that we have to discuss. By law, I have to report these types of incidents to Child Protective Services. What they'll do is come in, talk to you about your drug use, and then decide if you can, or cannot, keep your child.
(Joey gets up and walks out totally upset. Jenna leans forward placing her face in her hands and sobs.)

DR. TILL: Jenna, I'm sorry. Look at me.

(She slowly looks up at him.)

DR. TILL: You have the power to turn this whole thing around. You need to get some help, and get it now!
(Jenna sits up, takes a deep breath, wipes her eyes, and stands up.)

JENNA ALLEN: Can you help me?

DR. TILL: I'll check my resources and get back to you.

JENNA ALLEN: Thanks.

DR. TILL: Go on and get your husband, he needs you.
(Jenna leaves the office to find and Joey.)

TWENTY

(The next day, Devin is at a meeting with Mr. President. They're about to discuss that job Mr. President had mentioned he wanted Devin to do for him.)

MR. PRESIDENT: Devin, I want you to go with 187 down to Brook Heights, and take care of this fool down there that's trying to take over my corners.

DEVIN COX: You want us to rough him up and scare him a little?
(Mr. President and 187 look at each other and laugh.)

MR. PRESIDENT: First of all, there is no we. This is your job. Second of all, there is no game of scaring anybody. I want you to kill him.
(Devin's face goes blank.)

MR. PRESIDENT: Is there a problem?

DEVIN COX: Why do we have to kill the guy? Can't we just bang him up and scare him off?

MR. PRESIDENT: We have to kill the guy because I said so! And that's pretty much the end of this conversation. Go!
(Devin slowly stands up, and desperately wants to talk his way out of this job. But when Mr. President says a conversation is over, it's over. To prove their loyalty, and that they're in no way tied to law enforcement, every single one of his men have had to take a life. Devin is in no way a killer. But in the drug world, when you play the drug game, death becomes an experience, or a way of life. By the time Devin and 187 get to Brook Heights, Devin's hands are shaking so bad that it starts to bother 187.)

187: Man, you need to calm down! You're sitting over there shaking, acting like a little punk! This ain't no game boy! Now you need to get yourself together, get your mind right, and handle your business! You think Mr. President sent me all the way down here with you just for the ride? He sent me down here to put a bullet in your head, if you don't put one in his! (About that time, the guy they're looking for walks across the street right in front of them.)

187: There he is right there!
(The man walks behind an old condemned abandoned apartment building.)

187: You need to catch him while he's behind that building, take him out! Now go!
(All of the yelling has made the environment in the car so intense that you could cut it with a knife!)

DEVIN COX: Man, I don't know if I can do this!

(187 pulls out his gun.)

187: It's him or you!
(Devin takes a deep breath, opens the door, pauses before he gets out, and then takes off to do the job. After disappearing behind the building, 187 moves the car down the street a little putting the old building behind him just in case something goes wrong and he has to flee. He can now look in his rear view mirror and see the building. When Devin approaches the man behind the building, he thinks Devin is there to buy drugs.)

DEALER: What you need man?
(With his hands still shaking, Devin stands there with no response what so ever.)

DEALER: What's your problem, man? Do you want something or not?
(Devin's behavior begins to make the man very nervous.)

DEALER: Oh, you, 5.0?
(He thinks Devin is a cop. The dealer starts to slowly back up with all intentions of running. Sensing the man is going to make some kind of move, Devin draws his gun and aims it at the man's head. The man immediately raises his hands, and slowly falls to his knees.)

DEALER: Please don't kill me, man! Here!
(The dealer pulls out all of his money and drugs.)

DEALER: Take it, you can have it all! Please don't kill me, man. I just had my first child! Don't take me away from my son! I'm just out here trying to survive like everybody else!
(Devin starts to cry as the man begs and pleads for his life.)

DEALER: Please, man, don't do this, please!

DEVIN COX: If I don't I'm a dead man. They told me to get you off these corners.

DEALER: I'll leave! I'll leave and I won't come back I promise! (With his hand now holding a gun, and shaking out of control, Devin is forced to make a decision. Back in the car, 187 is getting a little impatient, and very nervous. He's done this type of thing many times, and he knows that this whole thing should have been over by now. Just as he looks down at his watch, he hears a gun shot. Thirty seconds later, Devin comes running towards the car. Still shaking, and still crying, he gets in on the passenger side, puts the gun on the floor, and weeps like a baby. 187 throws the car in gear and takes off down the street. Once they're on the highway heading home, he tries to calm Devin down.)

187: The first one is always the hardest, but it gets easier.

DEVIN COX: I'm not doing this anymore! He'll just have to kill me!

187: You don't have to worry about it. He didn't put you on the team to do this kind of stuff; that's my job. This was about loyalty, and commitment to him, and what we do.

(As true as those words are, they mean absolutely nothing to Devin. What's done is done. And what's done, is what he will have to live with for the rest of his life. His decision will be the very thing that will consistently return to haunt him, even in his dreams.)

TWENTY ONE

(A week or so after their emotional doctor's visit, Joey is at work trying to do his job. Leaving Jenna at home at night by herself worries him. He's afraid she'll go out and use. The stress of it all is obvious, especially to his assistant, Patrick Kerry.)

PATRICK KERRY: Joey, can I talk to you for a second?
(They walk into the break room and sit.)

PATRICK KERRY: Something's eating at you Joe, what's going on?
(Joey sits back in the chair, sighs, and starts to bounce his leg. Over time, Joey and Patrick have become pretty decent friends, so talking to Patrick doesn't make Joey uncomfortable.)

JOEY ALLEN: You wouldn't understand, Pat. I don't even understand it.

PATRICK KERRY: How about we give it a shot, what's up?
(Joey decides to tell him.)

JOEY ALLEN: My wife is pregnant, she's doing drugs, and they may take the baby away from us when it's born. That's what's eating at me, and I don't understand one bit of it. I don't understand how a woman can get pregnant, have a perfectly healthy baby, do drugs, and take that baby's health away. I just don't get it. She could kill our child.

PATRICK KERRY: That baby is not gonna die, you don't have to worry about that.

JOEY ALLEN: You don't know that. At this point anything can happen, especially if she does more drugs.

PATRICK KERRY: Joey, it doesn't matter what she does, that baby is good to go. God is not going to allow anything to happen to your child. He's the giver of life and death, not your doctor. Don't get me wrong, doctors have their place, but they don't have the power to call a life down. That's Jesus, He's the one that makes that decision.
(Joey shakes his head as he displays a little smirk on his face.)

JOEY ALLEN: Pat, I can appreciate your time, and you trying to help me along. But all of this God stuff and Jesus talk is not my thing. I don't believe it, I'm not interested in it, and to be honest with you, I don't want to hear it, no offense.

PATRICK KERRY: No, I'm not offended. I can respect what you're saying. I won't say anything else about it. I'll just let Jesus explain it to you.
(Joey laughs.)

JOEY ALLEN: You really believe all of that stuff don't you? You believe that there's this man sitting somewhere up in the sky, doing all of these things, and controlling everything that goes on down here?

PATRICK KERRY: Well, I don't believe God is sitting somewhere in the sky, but I do know He's sitting in heaven. And as far as Him controlling everything that goes on down here, I know He's left that up to us. It's called free will. Joey, your wife going out and doing drugs is not God's fault. I'm not judging her, I'm not being insensitive to your situation, and I'm certainly not trying to disrespect her. I'm just telling you the truth. She is making those decisions on her own, through her own free will. People are always crying about their rights to do what they want, and their freedom to choose! And when they abuse those two privileges, or take advantage of them, and things go wrong, God gets the blame.

JOEY ALLEN: I don't know anything about the Bible, but what I do know, is that this God of yours is supposed to be loving, and kind, and loves everybody. Now how can He, or She, because you really don't know for sure, if any of this stuff is even true. But, for the sake of argument, let's say it is. How can He or She be so loving, and just let all of this horrible stuff happen down here?

PATRICK KERRY: God has two wills. A perfect, and a permissive. His perfect will, is all of the things that He has ordained, and designed for our lives. His permissive will, is all of the things we desire outside of that. The perfect supplies your needs, and the permissive allows you to have all of your wants.

God takes full credit for one, and the responsibility of the other falls squarely on us.
(This fresh new truth that Joey has never heard, sparks his curiosity, and makes him think.)

PATRICK KERRY: As crazy as it sounds, these are some of the greatest times of your life Joey.
(Joey laughs hysterically.)

JOEY ALLEN: Now I know you're crazy! Did your boy up in the sky tell you that?
(Patrick smiles back at Joey.)

PATRICK KERRY: No, He didn't tell me that. But, He is gonna tell you.
(That bombshell truth hits Joey and immediately stops his laughter. He looks at Patrick as if he had just seen a ghost.)

PATRICK KERRY: We better get back to work.
(Patrick walks out ahead of Joey smiling all the way. He knows that God's word has once again done its job. There's a scripture in the bible that says, "God's word will never come back void." Patrick knows the impact that conversation has had on Joey. And he knows that's not the last God conversation he and Joey will have.

TWENTY TWO

(It's now three o'clock in the morning. Joey is at work on third shift, and Jenna is at home having the struggle of her life. The torture of craving drugs, is like sitting down in a chair, and surrounding yourself with ten thousand of the loudest, and most hateful people on the planet. And then all at once, those ten thousand people start screaming different things at the top of their lungs. Some are screaming you're going to die. Some are screaming your life is worth nothing. Some are screaming you have no future. Some are screaming the next hit will make you feel better. Some are screaming there's no way out of your addiction. All of them are lying at the same time, and while all of the screaming is going on, they're poking you all over your body as hard as they can. And while the screaming and the poking is going on, they hook every nerve in your body to a small electric probe, and shock you all at once, making you feel like you're about to lose your mind and only another fix, can solve your problem. You feel like you have to have another hit or you're gonna kill yourself. There is no in between when it comes to addiction and there's no limit, to what you're willing to do to silence the voices. It is one of the most evil experiences a human being could ever have. As hard as she tries, she just can't fight anymore. Jenna grabs her keys and heads for the door. Just as she's walking out, their little baby girl moves like she's never moved before. The movement in her stomach is so distinct, and so unusual, that it stops her in her tracks. She places her hand on the side of her belly and leans over. God is using that innocent little baby girl, to plead for her mother's life. But in spite of the warning from the womb, Jenna answers the call of addiction, and ignores the begging of her baby girl. Twenty minutes later Jenna is pulling up to a corner that's all too familiar to her. This particular corner is in a neighborhood that is run and controlled by the dealers that work for Devin. Jenna gets out of her car and walks over to a dealer they call, Black Jack.

BLACK JACK: Girl, I know you ain't out here thankin I'm selling you dope! It ain't even going down like that. What you doin out here pregnant killin that baby for anyway?

JENNA ALLEN: Please just one! Sell me just one and I'm done, please!

BLACK JACK: You need to get away from me girl! I ain't sellin you nothing, and ain't nobody else around here gonna sell you nothin!
(Jenna gets on her cell phone and calls Devin.)

JENNA ALLEN: Devin, I'm down here on Green Street trying to get something, and your guy won't sell it to me! He wants to talk to you!

DEVIN COX: Black!

BLACK JACK: Yeah!

DEVIN COX: What do you think you're doing man?

BLACK JACK: Man I'm not out here trying to sell no pregnant woman no dope man!

DEVIN COX: Look man, you're messing with my money! Now I don't care if she's pregnant, and pushing three more kids in a stroller! You're on that corner to sling my dope, not to have a conscience. Give her what she wants, or I'm coming down there! I'm not playin Black!
(Devin hangs up on him. Wanting to avoid dealing with an angry Devin, Black sells Jenna the drugs. As she's walking away, Black Jack yells,)

BLACK JACK: You a killer girl! A baby killer!
(In spite of her being satisfied with a score, Black's words penetrate down to the core of Jenna's being. She bursts into tears as she crosses the street and gets in her car. As soon as she takes off, her phone rings; it is Joey checking in on her. Jenna decides to ignore the call. She's afraid that he will pick up on something and know she's getting high. As soon as she sits down at the dining room table, she pulls out her razor, her straw, and snorts one of the biggest lines of cocaine she's ever done. She leans back in the chair and lets it all settle in. Joey is at work pacing and stressing because Jenna didn't answer her phone. So he pulls his phone out and tries her again. The ringing startles Jenna. She turns the volume down as fast as she can, the last thing she wants is to wake Jessica. But yet

again, she decides to ignore the call, as she dumps another small pile of cocaine on the table.)

JOEY ALLEN: Hey, Patrick!
(Patrick walks over to Joey.)

PATRICK KERRY: What's up?

JOEY ALLEN: I need to head home man! Jenna's not answering her phone, and I have a bad feeling that something is wrong.

PATRICK KERRY: That's fine, I can handle things here.

JOEY ALLEN: I appreciate it man, I owe you one.

PATRICK KERRY: Well, you can pay me what you owe me right now. Let me pray for you before you go.

JOEY ALLEN: Here, now?

PATRICK KERRY: Absolutely.
(Joey looks around to see if anybody can see them.)

JOEY ALLEN: Can we do it kinda quick?
(Seeing Joey's discomfort, Patrick is short and sweet with his prayer. All the way home Joey continues to call, and Jenna continues to ignore him. Jenna is now about to do her third huge line of cocaine. She grabs her straw, leans over, and takes another one. As she leans back in the chair, she feels an agonizing pain just below her belly button. The pain becomes so excruciating, that she can't even move. When she tries to stand up,

the pain drags her down to the floor, and her nose starts to bleed. She tries to call out to Jessica, but what's going on with her has paralyzed her voice. Jenna is slowly losing consciousness, and her nose is bleeding out of control. She's also starting to hemorrhage, and the baby is in serious trouble. Then it happens, she completely loses consciousness, lying in the middle of the floor, in her own blood. Joey finally gets home and when he walks in, what he finds causes him to scream. He runs over to her, puts his hands on her face, and repeatedly screams her name begging her to wake up. All of Joey's screaming yanks Jessica up out of her sleep. When she comes around the corner and sees Jenna lying there, she falls to the floor and starts to cry out Jenna's name.)

JOEY ALLEN: Jessica, Call 911!
(Shock has nailed Jessica's body to the floor.)

JOEY ALLEN: Jessica, call an ambulance!
(She doesn't move. Joey gently lays Jenna's head down and calls 911. Two hours later, Joey and Jessica are sitting in the waiting room waiting for the doctor. Jenna has been in the O.R. the whole time. Joey called Jenna's parents, and they're on their way to North Carolina from Tennessee.)

JOEY ALLEN: Jessica, I'm gonna go to the snack machine to get something to munch on. You want something?

JESSICA ALLEN: No, thank you.
(Joey kisses her on her head and walks off. As he's making his way to the snack machine, he looks up and sees a sign that reads Praying Chapel. Right away, the statement Patrick made

to him about God telling him that these are the best days of his life speaks for a second time. Joey stops, contemplates whether he's going to go in or not, and then decides the snack machine comes with less reality. After getting his snack, he makes his way back down the hall, all the while, hearing the Praying Chapel sign ask him, "why not?" One of the awesome things about God is that He will always make a way of escape. That way of escape will often be a way that we're not comfortable with, familiar with, or even feel necessary. We're all accountable for ourselves; that's where freewill places us: in a position of being responsible for our own decisions. If God were to take our freewill to choose, we would say "He's not fair, because He's controlling us." So to eliminate that excuse, He's given us freewill to choose. But when our choices end in pain, we once again look to heaven and tell God He's not fair. However, the awesome God we serve, is the God that will never leave us, nor forsake us. The tug of that Prayer Chapel on Joey's heart, in the end is victorious. He hesitantly walks inside. The only comfort he has, is the comfort of being the only one in the room. Down in front of the cross, there's a kneeling bench for prayer. Joey approaches the bench with extreme caution. He gets down on his knees, and has one of the most honest conversations he's ever had. He talks to God the only way he knows how.

JOEY ALLEN: I really don't know what I'm doing, and I really don't even know why I'm here. This talking to nothing stuff is strange to me. My friend, Patrick at work, is always talking about how great you are. He talks about how you take such good care of him and his family. To be honest, I don't believe you're real. And if you are, you seem kind of cruel to me.

There are people doing all kinds of bad things in this world, and all you seem to do is make them rich, or give them power. I don't get you. But I do get this situation I'm in, and I understand it's bad.
(Joey begins to cry.)

JOEY ALLEN: I've always been a good person, and I think it's a little unfair what's happening to me. There are two beautiful people down the hall suffering. And one is an innocent child.
(He wipes the tears running down his face with his sleeve.)

JOEY ALLEN: I don't know how all of this is going to turn out, but right now it looks real bad. If you're real, I need you to show me. If you're as great as people say you are, I need you to be good to me today. Reveal yourself to me! Today, here, in this hospital, for me! I want to see you!
(Joey drops his head and breaks down crying. As his tears continue to fall, Jessica walks in.)

JESSICA ALLEN: Joey.
(Jessica gently places her hand on his back.)

JESSICA ALLEN: You okay?

JOEY ALLEN: Yeah, I'm fine.

JESSICA ALLEN: The doctor wants to see you.
(As they are coming up the hall, Joey and Jenna's doctor, Dr. Till directs them into a little room to talk in private.)

JOEY ALLEN: So, how are they?

DR. TILL: When Jenna got here, her blood pressure was dangerously high. We tried a few things, and we were able to somewhat stabilize it. When we checked on the baby, we notice that the baby's heart rate was extremely high. At that point, we had to induce labor for the baby's sake. During the delivery, Jenna's blood pressure spiked again, and she had a massive stroke.

(Joey and Jessica both break down.)

JOEY ALLEN: Is she gonna be okay?

DR. TILL: We lost her Joe.

(Jessica immediately starts screaming, and Joey falls to his knees. The wailing and crying is too much for Dr. Till to handle. He's lost patients before, but Joey and Jenna had a very special place in his heart. He broke the rule and got a little too close to them, and now he's feeling the weight of the loss. As Dr. Till is walking out of the room, he sees Jenna's parents standing at the emergency check-in desk, frantically asking all sorts of questions. He met her parents once before when they came to town to visit Joey and Jenna. Dr. Till is not looking forward to the conversation he knows he's about to have. He sighs, and looks down at the floor. Dr. Till takes one deep breath, and walk up to the emergency room check-in desk. As soon as Jenna's parents spot him, they rush towards him with a flood of questions.)

DR. TILL: Can we please step into this office for a few minutes? I'll tell you everything that's going on.

(Dr. Till tries to take them to a different room. He doesn't want the initial news of what's happened to come from what they'll see if they see Joey. But Dr. Till's effort is short lived. From down the hall, they hear Joey screaming, "Jenna please don't die!" Jenna's mother, Betty Woods, immediately picks up on that voice.)

BETTY WOODS: Was that Joey?
(Betty takes off running towards his voice. Jenna's dad, Jeff Woods, grabs Dr. Till by his arm and gets right in his face.)

JEFF WOODS: I want you to tell me what's going on before I get down there, and I want you to tell me now!

DR. TILL: Jenna had a massive stroke during delivery and she died.

JEFF WOODS: What about the baby?

DR. TILL: The baby's in ICU.

JEFF WOODS: And?

DR. TILL: It's gonna take a miracle, we've done all that we can do. Between the drug use, the hemorrhage, and the strain Jenna put on her system, that baby's experienced as much stress as a full grown adult.
(Jeff slowly lets go of his arm. As he's looking directly into Dr. Till's eyes in absolute shock, he hears his wife screaming from down the hall. Jeff slowly makes his way down the hall to comfort his wife. As soon as he walks in, she almost falls into his arms. Dr. Till takes a seat off to the side and waits, just in case there are any questions. A few hours later, after they've all had

their time alone to say goodbye to Jenna, Joey gets his turn. The rest of the family is in the waiting room outside of the ICU. At first, Joey stands at a distance and just stares at her. With tears in his eyes, he makes his way over to her bed. He pulls up a chair, grabs her hand, and breaks down again.)

JOEY ALLEN: Jenna, I'm so sorry if this is my fault. People who do drugs are doing it to mask pain. If you had pain in your heart, and I put it there, I'm so sorry.
(He can hardly sit up straight.)

JOEY ALLEN: I love you so much. I don't know how I'm gonna leave you here. I know you fought with all you had. I know you fought for that sweet little girl. I'm so proud of you Jen, you're a great mom. No, you're the best mom in the world. And if our baby lives through this, that's all she'll ever know about you. She'll know she had the best mom in the world. She'll know that her mom loved her more than anything. And she'll know that her awesome mother died, so that she could live. I'm really, really proud of you Jenna. Joey lays his head on her hand that he's holding. Out of nowhere, Joey feels a hand on his shoulder. He turns around to see who it is, and standing there looking as healthy as he's ever looked, is Joey's dad. He can't believe his eyes. There in front of him, stands his alcoholic dad, completely sober and looking great. He's lost weight, his skin looks healthy, and he's got a glow about him. Joey stands up to face him.)

WALTER ALLEN: Son, the first thing I want to say is, I'm sorry about Jenna. And the second thing I want to say, is that I'm sorry about what I've done to you and Jessica.

(His dad starts to cry, which in turn makes Joey cry.)

WALTER ALLEN: Please forgive me, son.
(Joey wraps his arms around his dad, and loves on him for the first time in his life. What a beautiful moment. In spite of all that's happened, God showed up, and revealed instant proof, that He is a God of redemption, repair, and restoration. He has taught everybody a very valuable lesson, and that lesson is this: just because you don't see God doing it, doesn't mean it's not being done.)

WALTER ALLEN: I love you, Joey.

JOEY ALLEN: I know, dad.
(HEALED)
(The next day, the whole family makes their way back to the hospital to see how the baby's doing. As they're waiting to go in and see her, Joey's friend Patrick from work stops by. Joey introduces him to everybody, gives him a hug, and thanks him for coming by.

PATRICK KERRY: So how are you?

JOEY ALLEN: A little numb. And I can't find the words to explain the rest.

PATRICK KERRY: So, are they letting you guys in to see the baby?

JOEY ALLEN: Yeah, only two at a time.

PATRICK KERRY: Would you mind if I went in with you? I'd like to pray over her.

JOEY ALLEN: I appreciate it, but that won't be necessary. I tried that already.
(Patrick's eyes grow wide. He can't believe what he's hearing.)

JOEY ALLEN: I went in to the Prayer Chapel to pray for Jenna, and ten minutes later she was dead. So it's just like I said, it doesn't work. At least it didn't for me.

PATRICK KERRY: Can I pray over her anyway?
(Joey sighs. But because he likes Patrick, and he knows Patrick means well, he lets him go in with him.)

JOEY ALLEN: If it'll make you feel better.

PATRICK KERRY: Joey, a whole lot of good is going to come out of this. And you'll see it.
(Joey looks over at his dad.)

PATRICK KERRY: Who's that?

JOEY ALLEN: That's my dad.
(Joey smiles. He so proud of his father.)

PATRICK KERRY: Wait, is this the alcoholic father you can't stand the sight of?

JOEY ALLEN: He doesn't drink anymore. He went into treatment, and he's been sober for eight months. I'm really proud

of him. We stayed up pretty much all night talking, well, he did most of the talking. It was really good. And you want to hear something funny? When you complete the program, they assign you a sponsor. Kinda like an accountability partner. He and his sponsor have become pretty good friends. They fish, get together for football games, and on Sundays, believe it or not, he goes to church with this guy.
(Patrick smiles.)

JOEY ALLEN: His sponsor is Jenna's dad. He was an alcoholic once, and when they got pregnant with Jenna, he got some help and quit drinking. He's been sober for twenty-six years.

PATRIC KERRY: Can you see the pattern, Joey? You see that spirit of addiction that sits around and waits for its opportunity to attack? It attacked Jenna's father, it probably attacked his father, and it got Jenna. But in the name of Jesus, it will not get that baby!

JOEY ALLEN: Looks like it already has.

PATRICK ALLEN: No, the baby's fine. What's going on with the baby right now has nothing to do with the baby. This is about everybody else. See Joey, Jesus has already begun that baby's ministry. Your little girl has a calling on her life. God is going to use her to restore relations of all kinds. Look around you Joe. Look at your little girl's ministry! She's doing pretty good so far.
(Joey looks at the family and smiles.)

JOEY ALLEN: My mom is back home in Tennessee in treatment right now. Her and my dad are both getting help with their drinking. They're in marriage counseling and doing pretty good. He said they don't want to do to the baby, what they did to my sister and me.

PATRICK FERRY: Healing relationships Joe. That's her gift.
(Joey and Patrick go in and Patrick prays over the baby. He pulls a little bottle of oil out of his pocket.)

JOEY ALLEN: What's that?

PATRICK KERRY: It's anointing oil. I'd like to rub a little bit on the baby's head.

JOEY ALLEN: What's it for?

PATRICK KERRY: Healing, and victory.
(Patrick rubs the oil on the baby's forehead and prays.)

PARTICK KERRY: In the mighty name of Jesus! I declare and decree victory over this beautiful baby's life! In the name of Jesus, I speak life over this child's future, over this child's ministry, and over this child's soul! In the name of Jesus, I bind and rebuke the spirit of addiction! Satan, you cannot, and you will not, have this baby, or this baby's future! Jesus, use the blood you shed on Calvary to cover this baby, this family, and their relationships. And Jesus, I personally want to thank you for saving Joey's soul! Thank you for his salvation, and the ministry you've already prepared for him. Give him a heart of forgiveness, and set him free from all of his hurt and pain!

(A tear runs down Joey's face.)

PATRICK KERRY: It is in the Holy name of Jesus Christ I pray, amen!
(Joey wipes his eyes.)

PATRICK KERRY: The Lord wanted me to tell you, that in the next seven weeks, not only will your daughter be home, but she'll be completely healed. He said don't believe everything these doctors are telling you. It's final, and she's free, forever! You can watch her every day of her life, and you'll never ever know her mother did drugs. God's not going to leave you with that! When you look at the beautiful child, He's gonna make sure you always see the beauty of your wife. That's Jesus!
(Joey steps forward and gives him a hug. Patrick, and what he brings to Joey's life, is like nothing Joey has ever seen, and what perfect timing. God said that with everything, there is a time and a season. Sometimes we feel like some of our life seasons will never change or get better. We feel like we're never going to exit our suffering, or enter our rest. We allow life to convince us that peace of mind is the rabbit, and we're the turtle. But, if you remember that story, that old turtle caught that rabbit. God said He would never leave us, nor forsake us. But He never said that we wouldn't hurt. We should never expect life to treat us better than it treated Jesus. After about two more months in the hospital, Dr. Till finally clears the baby to go home. They've done test after test, and every one of them came back positive. She got exactly what Jesus promised her, she got her healing. She is as healthy as they come. Joey decided to wait until he could take her home before he would reveal her name to the rest of the family. They were

all sitting in the waiting room waiting for Dr. Till to release her, including Joey's mom. She made it through treatment and has been sober for three months. She looks great, and she feels like she's finally living for the first time.)

BETTY WOODS: All right Joey, today she's coming home, so can you tell us what you named her?
(Joey smiles)

JOEY ALLEN: I named her Lilly.
(Jenna's mom, Betty, starts to cry.)

BETTY WOODS: That was Jenna's favorite flower.

JOEY ALLEN: Jenna would have loved that name.
(Dr. Till and two nursery nurses arrive with Lilly. When they hand her to Joey, his emotions take over and he starts to cry. His tears set off tears all over the room. Even Dr. Till is crying.)

JOEY ALLEN: Dr. Till, I can't thank you enough for all that you've done for me. You're a great man, and you're a great doctor.
(Dr. Till pulls his handkerchief out to wipe his eyes. Then he hugs Joey and whispers in his ear.)

DR. TILL: I love my job because of people like you.
(After they hug, the rest of the family takes turns holding her. In that room, is enough love to last Baby Lilly her entire life and then some. After getting home and putting Lilly to sleep, Joey starts the process of gathering Jenna's things together.

Jenna's parents are coming over from their hotel to make dinner, and Joey wants them to go through Jenna's things and take whatever sentimental things they want. As he's putting stuff together, he sees her cell phone under the table. He picks it up, presses the power button, and gets nothing. He plugs it into the charger, turns it on, and notices she's got eight missed calls. So he goes into her phone log, and sees that all of the calls are from Devin. He doesn't think much about it at first. He thinks that maybe he was calling because of everything that's happened. He saw Devin at the funeral, but they didn't get a chance to talk a lot. But then he notices something strange. He looks at the date of some of Jenna's other calls, and notices that she called Devin, and had a four minute conversation with him a couple of hours before she died. Joey grabs his phone and calls Devin.)

DEVIN COX: Joe Joe! How are you man?

JOEY ALLEN: I don't know yet. Let me ask you something, when was the last time you spoke to Jenna before she died?

DEVIN COX: About three days after my party I think. She texted me a couple of times to ask me how my mom was doing but that was about it. Why?

JOEY ALLEN: I checked her phone log, and it says that she made a call to your phone at 10:15p.m. the night she died. Now why is that?

DEVIN COX: She may have called, but I didn't talk to her.

JOEY ALLEN: You're lying again, Devin, and you're ticking me off. She talked to you for four minutes. There was cocaine all over the table when I got home, and I found her on the floor in a pool of her own blood. Now, I'm gonna ask you one more time, do you know who she got the drugs from?
(With Devin knowing Joey as well as he does, he knows that Joey is not going to leave this whole thing alone until he gets the result he wants. And the last thing Devin wants or needs, is Joey of all people, kicking up dust and Mr. President finding out.)

DEVIN COX: All right. She went out to buy a little something, and my boy wouldn't sell it to her, so she called me to straighten it out.

JOEY ALLEN: You're a drug dealer, Devin?

DEVIN COX: I'm a business man, son!

JOEY ALLEN: Did you ever sell her drugs yourself?

DEVIN COX: No, but I gave her some. Gave her a few other things too.
(Devin laughs.)

JOEY ALLEN: You killed my wife, Devin. My wife and your friend.

DEVIN COX: Look Joey, is there something else you want, man? Because I don't have time for all of this nonsense!

JOEY ALLEN: Yeah, there is something else I want. I want you dead.

DEVIN COX: The only thing between us is air and opportunity. When you want to man up, and play that game, then come get me. I saved your life that day in the restaurant when my man wanted to smoke you. But who's gonna save you from me?

JOEY ALLEN: I'll tell my daughter you said thank you. Because Devin, if it wasn't for her, I'd kill you. That baby not dying is what's keeping you alive. Strange isn't it? As you were giving my wife poison to kill her, she was giving me a child to save you. I don't ever want to hear from you, see you, or ever have anything to do with you again. And if you come anywhere near my family again, nothing's gonna save you. You're a dead man, Devin!
(Joey hangs up, with all intentions of never hearing from Devin again. But chance and opportunity are going to come face to face, bringing these two new enemies together again. As a year dashes by, life is really starting to settle down for Joey. He's in a very good daddy routine with Baby Lilly, and is doing quite well as a single father. Having Jessica in the house has been a real help. Baby Lilly's ministry continues on. Jessica is like a new person. She's on honor roll at school, she's captain of her softball team, and she's an amazing Aunt Jess. She and her parents talk a couple times a week. Although there's still a lot of work to be done on their relationship, everybody is in a good place of willingness to do their part. But things in Devin's life are about to take a horrible turn. Mr. President's hit man, 187, is taking his twelve year old son to Harvest Fest in the neighboring town. It's a family festival he's been attending

since he was a child. As he's walking around checking out all of the games and food trucks, he just happens to look to his left and what he sees makes him do a double take. He tells his son to come with him, and he hurries off to make sure he was seeing what he thought he saw, and there it was. He absolutely could not believe it. Standing fifteen feet away watching his daughter ride the merry go round, is the guy Mr. President sent Devin out to get rid of a little over a year ago, because he thought the guy was trying to take over his territory. Instead of shooting the guy, Devin let him go. He couldn't bring himself to shoot another human being. He gave the guy a hand full of cash, and told him to leave town and start life over somewhere else, and that's what the guy did. But he didn't go very far. He's actually doing well. He stopped selling drugs, got a job, and got married. His near death experience with Devin was enough. 187 cautiously positions himself to take a picture of the guy with his phone. After taking the photo, he calls Mr. President.)

MR. PRESIDENT: What's up?

187: I need to meet with you right away!

MR. PRESIDENT: Something wrong?

187: Yeah! It's bad, real bad!

MR. PRESIDENT: Meet me at my office in one hour!

187: Cool.

(One hour later when he sits down at the table with Mr. President, he hands him his phone.)

MR. PRESIDENT: Ok, you have a picture of somebody we got rid of. What's the problem?

187: The problem is that I took this picture a little over an hour ago, sixteen miles from here in the town of Bilton! My son and I were hanging out at the Family Harvest Fest, I looked around, and there he was. Alive and well hanging out with his kids at the merry-go-round.
(Mr. President sits back in his chair and stares at the picture.)

MR. PRESIDENT: Are you sure it's the same guy?
(Mr. President hopes it's a mistake, because if it's not, Devin will have to go. There are some things he can let Devin get away with. But blatantly disobeying an order such as this one, is an absolute no no.)

187: How do you want me to handle it?
(Mr. President takes a deep breath. He really is struggling with this. He knows there's only one thing he can do, he has to get rid of Devin.)

MR. PRESIDENT: Give me twenty-four hours, and I'll let you know when to get rid of him.
(It has now been established. There's absolutely no way he can turn back now. In the next twenty-four hours, twenty six-year-old Devin Allen Cox, will join the list of those gone too soon.

TWENTY THREE

(The hands of time have done their job. Twenty-four hours have passed, and the day has arrived. Mr. President calls a mandatory meeting.)

MR. PRESIDENT: A while back, 1 sent Devin out to handle somebody for me. Well that somebody was seen walking around in the town of Bilton yesterday. Now as much as 1 hate to do it, because of the money he brings in every month, Devin has got to go. What he did could have gone in another direction and got all of us killed. What if this guy was a part of one of these little clicks that pop up every now and then to take some of my business? We would all be dead by now. Orders are to be followed, not felt. We don't do emotions, we do business! None of us can afford to have a conscience. 187, 1'm gonna ask him to meet on the fourth level parking deck of my Salem Street Center Building around eight tomorrow. 1 want you to hang out somewhere close, and when you see him park and turn off his lights, go in and do what you do. Then 1 want you to drive him out somewhere, dump him, and get rid of the car. 1 don't want that car found by anybody, ever! Do you understand that?

187: Consider it done.

(After the meeting, Mr. President dismisses all of the guys. After they're all gone he gets up and pours himself a drink. Killing Devin is eating at his soul, and he just can't seem to shake it. He's ordered hits many times, but this time it's different. This time it's somebody he really cares about. They've become pretty close over the last few years. All night he tossed and turned. One time during the night he woke up in a cold sweat. It's almost as if something was haunting him and he knew it. Back home in Tennessee, at the exact same time of Mr. President's torture, Devin's mother, Mama Lucy, has taken every single picture of Devin in the house, and put them in the Bible. She's been up fasting and praying over that Bible for almost ten hours straight. She vowed to God, that if she had to die fasting to save her baby, then she would. She told God during her prayers, that if she has to, she'd wrestle with Him longer and harder than Jacob could have ever imagined. She knows something is wrong in North Carolina with her son, but she doesn't ask and she doesn't stress. She just prays and believes. It's now 6:15 the next night, 1-hour and 45 minutes before the hit. Mr. President does something extremely unusual, something he hasn't done in 10 years.)

187: Hello.

MR. PRESIDENT: Hey, man, that job 1 gave you to do yesterday, don't worry about it. I'm gonna take care of it myself.
(187 can't believe what he's hearing.)

187: You're gonna do it?

MR. PRESIDENT: Yeah, I've got this one.
(187 is speechless.)

187: Are you sure you don't want me to take care of it?

MR. PRESIDENT: Na, it's all good. I need this one for myself.

187: All right, if you say so. If you change your mind call me.

MR. PRESIDENT: You know I will.
(He hangs up the phone, and leaves to meet Devin. After watching Devin park his car and turn off his lights, Mr. President quietly walks up behind his car, and scares Devin by banging on the trunk. Devin yanks out his gun and jumps out of the car.)

DEVIN COX: Oh, it's you!
(Devin takes a deep breath.)

DEVIN COX: You almost got shot sneaking up on me like that!

MR. PRESIDENT: Caught you off guard didn't I? Always back into a parking space up against the parking deck wall. Then that way nobody can sneak up on you.

DEVIN COX: Next time I'll know. So what's up, why did you want to meet me here?

MR. PRESIDENT: I wanted to introduce you to somebody.
(Mr. President pulls a picture of the guy Devin was supposed to kill out of his pocket and hands it to him.)

DEVIN COX: This is the guy I smoked a few months ago.

MR. PRESIDENT: Game recognizes game, Devin. Not only are you lying to me, you're insulting my intelligence. I know you didn't handle that! So you need to stop while you're ahead!
(Mr. President is getting angry.)

MR. PRESIDENT: Now I'm gonna ask you one time. Did you do him?

DEVIN COX: No. I couldn't.

MR. PRESIDENT: You should have!

DEVIN COX: I'm not a killer! I'll make you all the money you want! But, I can't kill another human being! I don't have it in me!

MR. PRESIDENT: So what am I supposed to do right now, Devin? If I let you get away with this, I will lose every bit of respect I've earned! And I'm not willing to throw that away for you or anybody else! If I let you walk, I'd be dead in a week. My own guys would spot the weakness and take me out! That's how this business works, Devin!
(Mr. President pulls out his gun.)

MR. PRESIDENT: Put your gun on the ground!
(Devin slowly places his gun on the ground.)

MR. PRESIDENT: Get in the car!
DEVIN COX: Please, don't do this!

MR. PRESIDENT: I said get in the car!
(Devin gets in.)

MR. PRESIDENT: Close the door!
(Devin closes the door.)

DEVIN COX: Don't make my mother bury me, man, please!
(Mr. President opens fire and starts shooting into the car. After unloading nine shots, Devin is left slumped over in the driver's seat bleeding from every part of his body. Mr. President flags a white van across the parking lot to come over. Four guys get out.)

MR. PRESIDENT: Wrap him up and get him out of here!
(After they get Devin into the van, one of the three guys drives Devin's car away following the white van. Just another senseless tragedy that will never be explained. Two years have now gone by. Baby Lilly is almost four, Jessica is a senior in high school, and Joey is now Senior Supervisor of the Software Development Department. Family relationships have gotten better, single fatherhood has gotten better, but the anger and hatred for Devin remains. Joey's assistant Patrick Kerry has moved up the corporate ladder right along with Joey. They've become best friends over the last three years. With the friendship, has come the never-ending verbal vendetta that Joey carries in his heart. Over the years, Patrick has tried to help Joey understand two things. One, forgiveness is the only place he's going to find rest from all of the damage Devin has done. And two, only Jesus can supply that rest. But, Joey's not buying either. Even after hearing of Devin getting shot, and nobody ever finding him, he still can't shake the resentment.

Two more years go by, Baby Lilly is entering first grade, Jessica is in her sophomore year of college on a softball scholarship, and life is pretty good. Joey's parents have moved to North Carolina and are still sober. They joined an AA support group at one of the local churches. Although they don't go to church every Sunday, and are still very doubtful about Christianity, God has surrounded them with a good core group of believers that refuse to walk away and give up on them. As Joey is sitting in the car pool line waiting to pick up Baby Lilly, his phone rings. It's Patrick.)

PATRICK KERRY: I scored two tickets to the Masters in two weeks! If I jump on them now, I can land a free townhouse to go along with them that's twenty minutes from the course. Maybe you can leave Lilly with Jenna's parents since they don't get to see her that often and we can slide on down to Augusta, Georgia.

JOEY ALLEN: I'm in! I'll call Jenna's folks right now!

PATRICK KERRY: Call me back as soon as you get it straightened out!

JOEY ALLEN: I'll call you right back!
(Joey calls Jenna's parents. Without hesitation, they agree to keep Baby Lilly for a couple of days. He calls Patrick, and they begin to plan their big golf weekend.)

TWENTY FOUR

(Two weeks later, as they enter the small town Joey grew up in, a flood of memories come back. He can't help but think about Jenna, and all the good times they had as kids. Then his memories of Devin kick in, and the atmosphere in the car changes right away. Patrick can tell something is bothering him.)

PATRICK KERRY: You all right?
(Joey doesn't answer.)

PATRICK KERRY: You don't like it here do you?

JOEY ALLEN: Now you see why I never come back here. I hate this place. All of the drama I went through with my parents, my memories of Jenna. And the saddest part of it all, is that every time I think about Jenna, I can't help but to think about Devin because of what he did. Take a left right here!
(Joey has decided to take Baby Lilly to her mother's grave site for the first time. When they reach the plot where Jenna is buried, Joey gets down on one knee.)

JOEY ALLEN: Baby, when mommy died, we brought her back down here to bury her.

BABY LILLY: Why?

JOEY ALLEN: Well, this is where mommy grew up, and this is where she said she wanted to be buried when she died.

BABY LILLY: Daddy, was mommy funny?
(Joey's face lights up with a huge smile.)

JOEY ALLEN: She was hilarious! I remember the very first joke mommy told me when we were nine years old on the playground at school. You want to hear it?

BABY LILLY: Yes.

JOEY ALLEN: What kinds of beans don't grow in a garden?

BABY LILLY: I don't know.

JOEY ALLEN: Jelly beans!
(Baby Lilly laughs.)

BABY LILLY: Mommy was silly!
(Lilly looks down at the head stone, and there's a brief moment of silence.)

BABY LILLY: Did mommy love me daddy?
(Joey starts to cry.)

JOEY ALLEN: She loved you so much Lilly! When you were in her belly, she made up love songs and sang them to you all the time. She loved you more than anything!

BABY LILLY: Then why did she die and go away?
(Joey just can't hold it together. He drops his head and cries.)

BABY LILLY: Daddy, I'm sorry I made you sad.

JOEY ALLEN: You didn't make me sad honey. I just miss mommy that's all.

BABY LILLY: I told my friend Lauren at school that my mommy had died, and you know what she said to me?

JOEY ALLEN: What baby?

BABY ALLEN: She said Jesus could take me to her to see her one day. Is that true daddy?
(Patrick is standing behind them. Joey looks back at Patrick, and then turns back to Lilly.)

JOEY ALLEN: I don't know honey, I'm not sure. How about you say good bye to mommy so we can get you to Papa and Mimi's house?

BABY LILLY: Bye, mommy. I'm sorry you had to die and go away. I'm gonna talk to my friend Lauren at school, and ask her how I can get to Jesus. And when I get His phone number, I'll get daddy to call Him because I don't know how to use a phone yet.

(Joey cries through the whole conversation.)

BABY LILLY: I have a picture of you beside my bed. But, you already know that, because we talk every night! How could I forget that!
(Lilly starts laughing. She turns to Joey with that big beautiful smile.)

BABY LILLY: I'm silly! Daddy, I'm silly like mommy!

JOEY ALLEN: You are baby.

BABY LILLY: I have to go now mommy to see Papa and Mimi. I'll see you later!
(As only a child can, Lilly says her good-byes, grabs her daddy's hand, and just walks away from her mother's grave as if she had never had the experience at all. Only the heart of a child could carry that much freedom and peace. After Joey and Patrick get settled in, and have some dinner, everybody gathers together out on the screened in porch on a beautiful southern spring day.

PATRICK KERRY: Joey, what do you think about getting a hotel tonight, and taking off first thing in the morning? I'd like to hang out and relax and get a fresh start in the morning if that's all right with you?

JOEY ALLEN: It doesn't matter to me.

JEFF WOODS: Well if you're going to stay, you most certainly are not going to do it in a hotel! You're gonna stay right here, and that's final!

JOEY ALLEN: You okay with that, Pat?

PATRICK KERRY: Perfect.

BETTY WOODS: Perfect is right. You couldn't have picked a better night to be here! Tonight is our final night of revival!
(Patrick pops up in his chair.)

PATRICK KERRY: Wait, what? Did you say revival?

BETTY WOODS: It's the last night!

PATRICK KERRY: I'm in! Joe, you in?

JOEY ALLEN: I think I'll just hang out here with Lilly and watch a movie or something.

JEFF WOODS: Well, we were going to take her to church anyway, so you might as well go.
(Joey looks at Patrick.)

PATRICK KERRY: Come on, Joe! It's revival man!
(Joey pauses.)

JOEY ALLEN: All right I'll go.

PATRICK KERRY: My man! Have you ever been to a revival?

JOEY ALLEN: No.

PATRICK ALLEN: It's awesome Joe! Who's tonight's speaker?

JEFF WOODS: It's a Pastor from Texas, Pastor Evan Wright.
(At six thirty, they get in their cars and head off to the revival. The church is starting to get packed. They manage to get a decent seat on the seventh pew from the front. Joey, being the smart father he is, sits on the end of the pew next to the aisle, just in case Lilly has to go to the bathroom. As the program gets under way, you can just feel the excitement and energy in the building. After one of the members of the church gives a very warm welcome from the pulpit, a young woman sits down and begins to gently play the keyboards. A woman sitting behind Joey stands up and whispers, "Thank you Jesus," over and over.)

JOEY ALLEN: You see, that's the kind of stuff I just don't understand. This lady starts playing, and this lady behind us starts talking to Jesus. What is that all about?
(As Joey continues to talk, the young lady playing the keyboards starts singing. Her beautiful voice captures the attention of everybody in the church except for Joey. He's still complaining about everything that's going on around him.)

JOEY ALLEN: This is why I refuse to go to these things. I don't know why I agreed to come here.
(Patrick points towards the young lady singing.)

PATRICK KERRY: That's why you're here!

(Joey looks up at the young lady, and there in front of him, sitting in a wheelchair fifteen feet away on the stage is Devin. He cannot believe his eyes. He can't believe that Devin is actually right in front of him. Joey is completely at a loss for words, and he's immediately overcome by rage. He starts to gather Lilly's things to leave.)

 (He leans over to Patrick.)

JOEY ALLEN: Did you know anything about this?

PATRICK KERRY: Yes. I've been talking with Jenna's parents for the last few months. When they called me and told me that Devin was back in Tennessee, I knew what God was doing. Devin was shot nine times, and he lived. Nine times, Joey! His survival was for him, but it's about you!
(Joey looks at Devin.)

PATRICK KERRY: Joey, you're gonna have to forgive him. That hatred you have in your heart, eventually, it's going to make its way to your daughter's heart. Our kids are affected by everything we do and say. You want her to have the same black hole in her heart that you do? Do you, Joey? Because that's exactly what's going to happen! It may not be for Devin, but it will be for somebody, or something. In God's eyes, Joe, doing that to our children is the same as shedding innocent blood.
(A tear rolls down his face.)

JOEY ALLEN: He took Jenna away from me, Patrick. I don't know how to forgive him.

PATRICK KERRY: You may have lost Jenna, but look what you got in return. Look at your baby.
(Joey looks at Lilly, and kisses her on the forehead.)

PATRICK KERRY: What a beautiful exchange.
(Devin wheels himself up to the microphone. One of the shots Mr. President fired skimmed his spinal cord, leaving him paralyzed from the waist down. He lost most of the use of his right arm, and his memory can sometimes be hit or miss. But the one thing he'll never forget, is how to sing. Just as his wife, the beautiful young lady playing the keyboards finishes singing, it's Devin's turn. Just before he starts, he spots Joey sitting in the audience. He can't move, he can't sing, and he can't help but to cry. The regret that tortures him daily now has a visual face. But, it's not Joey's face that's making him so emotional. It's that sweet Baby Lilly that gets him. Looking at Lilly is like looking at Jenna all over again. He can't shake the guilt of what he did that caused that little girl to lose her mother. Joey and Devin lock eyes. Both are crying, both are hurting, and both are holding the keys to each other's prison. Devin swallows the lump in his throat, and tries to gather himself. He looks to his left, and sitting there on the front row, is his mother, good old Mama Lucy, smiling back at him.)

DEVIN COX: When I was in the hospital, after being shot nine times, I had a lot of time to think. I was in a coma for six weeks, and when I came out of it, I had no idea who, or where I was. When I was well enough to be transferred down here, it hit me. I was back where I started, to start all over again. I didn't know who my mother was when she walked into the room. But somehow, some way, I knew this one thing: Sometimes God has to take you back to where you started, to make you great. I saw that there was victory in my detour.

(The church erupts with praise. But this time, Joey's not complaining, and he's not asking questions. He's realizing that this Jesus he hears so much about is real. Devin's words flipped a switch in Joey's heart, and opened his eye to see beyond what is in his control. He's realizing that he's tired of being angry, and hateful, and he just wants some peace. Hating Devin has consumed his life so much to the point that he thinks that anybody who doesn't agree with him, is out to hurt him. Living life on the defensive all the time has emotionally worn him out.)

DEVIN COX: One day when I was laying in my hospital bed, I started to write down some words. Those words sounded something like this.

(Devin's wife begins to play, as Devin sings. Although Joey can hear him singing, it's the words that's causing his heart to change.)

DEVIN COX: God, I heard you whispering my name,
But I followed my flesh the other way.
I ignored your beckon call.
As my selfish desires controlled my day
Nothing else seemed to matter.
Even as I smelled my death in the air
I turned my back on what you were offering.
With the devil my soul I began to share.
Lost and tortured, I continued on my way.
My life was all about me.

I rejected your Son.
Then darkness fell.
And then finally you were all I could see.
You showed me what was to come.
And then showed me another way.
My way of escape you did provide.
And that's why I'm here today
To God be the glory.
Because of you Jesus.
Today I'm here, saved, and alive.
Thank you Jesus for not leaving me there.
Your blood is why I survived.

(Devin is so emotional, he barely gets through the song. When he's done, he drops his head and cries. With his face buried in his hands, he's looking down at the floor. Out of nowhere, a pair of shoes appear. He looks up, and there's Joey standing in front of him sobbing. Joey gets down on one knee so that they're eye to eye.)

DEVIN COX: Joe, 'I'm sorry' will never be enough.
(There isn't one dry eye in the entire church.)

DEVIN COX: I know I can never make things right man.

JOEY ALLEN: But I can.
(Joey extends his hand for Devin to shake.)

JOEY ALLEN: I forgive you, Devin.

(Devin can hardly believe it. So he asks Joey for the one thing Joey said he would never give him.)

DEVIN COX: Give me a hug, Joe. Hug me so I'll know.
(All their lives, from the time they first met, to that very moment, Joey had never ever hugged Devin. He said he would never hug another guy. The reason was because his dad had never hugged him and he wanted the first hug he got from a man to be from his dad. On the night Jenna died, Joey got that hug from his dad. Joey leans forward, and hugs his friend for the first time in his life.)

DEVIN COX: I'm so sorry, man. I'm so sorry!
(Joey's healing won't allow him to talk. He's finally free from it all. In that moment, Joey realizes that Patrick was right. What he was going through at the time, Jenna's death, his anger, and his sadness, was the best time of his life. God was transforming Joey into the great man he ordained him to be. Sometimes God has to allow your life to be completely dismantled, in order to rebuild you better. When we come out on the other side, we're stronger, wiser, humbled, and on the right path of life to happiness. After a very long and emotional embrace, they look at each other and laugh. God's miracle will do that to you sometimes. All you can do is laugh.

JOEY ALLEN: You're still as ugly as ever.

DEVIN COX: At least I'm prettier than you!
(The two old friends hug again. Devin sits back in his wheelchair and puts his hands on Joey's shoulders.)

DEVIN COX: Joey, do you believe that Jesus is the Son of God?

JOEY ALLEN: What?

DEVIN COX: Do you believe that Jesus Christ is the Son of God?
(Joey gets choked up.)

JOEY ALLEN: Yes.

DEVIN COX: Say it, Joey. Confess it with your mouth!
(Joey confesses it.)

DEVIN COX: Confess that you believe that He died on the cross and rose on the third day!
(Joey confesses it.)

DEVIN COX: Confess that you're a sinner.
(Joey confesses it.)

DEVIN COX: Ask Jesus to forgive you for your sins.
(Joey asks.)

DEVIN COX: Ask Jesus to come into your heart as your Lord and Savior.
(Joey asks.)

DEVIN COX: Joey!
(Joey looks up at Devin with tears in his eyes.)

DEVIN COX: You're saved, man! You have salvation. If Jesus walked into this church right now, no matter how long He stayed, when He left, He'd take you with Him. We're gonna spend eternity with Him Joe! How great is that?
(Lilly walks up on the stage to be with her dad.)

JOEY ALLEN: Devin, this is Lilly.
(Devin is speechless as he can only shake his head. He can't believe how much she looks like Jenna.)

DEVIN COX: Lilly, Jenna's favorite flower.

BABY LILLY: Hi, Mr. Devin
(He cries as he shakes her hand.)

DEVIN COX: Your mother was an amazing woman. Don't ever forget that.
(She gives him a hug. Lilly hugging him was like Jenna herself reaching from the grave and forgiving him. For the next four days, Patrick and Joey decide to hang out in Joey's hometown. They never made it to the Masters. Joey visited old friends, did some fishing, and had some awesome Bible time with Devin, Patrick, and Jenna's dad on the screened in porch. For the first time in a long time, Joey was truly enjoying life. The day He and Patrick left, later that night, Mama Lucy went to bed, and peacefully died in her sleep. When she died, she died with everything she needed. Devin was saved, he was safe, he was reconciled, things were restored, broken hearts were healed, and she had Jesus. She met her Savior lacking absolutely nothing. After getting back to North Carolina, and settling into life, Joey met a young lady at his gym. A year and a half-later, Joey

ask her to marry him, and she said yes. He was so excited, that he couldn't wait to get to work to tell Patrick. He walks into the break room looking for him and doesn't find him, so he asks Dave, the guy sitting in the break room if he's seen Patrick.)

DAVE: Who?

JOEY ALLEN: Come on man I don't have time for games! I really need to talk to him!

DAVE: I don't know who you're talking about.
(Joey gives up on Dave and looks elsewhere. He goes into his supervisor's office to ask him.)

JOEY ALLEN: Excuse me sir, have you seen Patrick?

SUPERVISOR: Who?

JOEY ALLEN: Oh so they've got you in on the joke too?

SUPERVISOR: Joey what are you talking about? I'm a little busy here in case you haven't noticed!

JOEY ALLEN: I'm trying to find Patrick! You know, my assistant manager, Patrick Kerry!

SUPERVISOR: Joey, I've been working here for twenty-six years! And I know for sure, that we've never had anybody named Patrick Kerry working here! Now if you don't mind, can you go look for your imaginary friend somewhere else?

JOEY ALLEN: But he's been here working with me for almost six years!

SUPERVISOR: Out of my office please!
(Joey leaves, closing the door behind him. He walks into his office and pulls up the staff info contact list. If you work for the company, your name is on that list. He scrolls down to the K's, and looks for the name Kerry. And to his amazement, there is no Patrick Kerry. He calls down to Human Resources.

JOEY ALLEN: Jill!

JILL: Hi, Joey!

JOEY ALLEN: Jill, I'm trying to find Patrick Kerry on the employee contact list, and it's not showing up anywhere.

JILL: There's nobody by that name that works here.

JOEY ALLEN: There has to be!

JILL: I've been dealing with every employee in this company for almost nine years, and I've never heard of any Patrick Kerry.

JOEY ALLEN: Okay. Thanks, Jill.
(Joey doesn't get it. Then he has a great idea. He calls Jenna's parents.)

BETTY WOODS: Hello!

JOEY ALLEN: Hi, Betty.

BETTY WOODS: Joey! How are you, son?

JOEY ALLEN: I'm good, but I'm a little confused about something. Do you remember the friend that came with me to drop Lilly off the weekend we were going to go to the Masters?

BETTY WOODS: Jonathan? Of course I do! He was a sweet young man, why?

JOEY ALLEN: Betty, I'll call you back.
(Joey's so flustered, that he hangs up on Jenna's mother. He gets up and walks to Patrick's office. When he gets there, he walks in without knocking.)

JONATHAN: Joey! What's up?

JOEY ALLEN: You're Jonathan?
(Jonathan frowns at him. He's a little caught off guard and confused.)

JONATHAN: Yeah.

JOEY ALLEN: What's your job here?

JONATHAN: I'm your assistant manager.

JOEY ALLEN: How long have you been my assistant?

JONATHAN: Right at six years.

(Joey turns around and walks out. He stops by his supervisor's office and tells him that he's going to work from home today. As Joey's driving, he's trying to figure out what in the world is going on. He's so confused. He begins to almost zone out thinking about it. All of a sudden, there's a man standing in the road holding a stop sign. They're doing construction on the road, and Joey's normal route home is shut down. He has to take a detour, which sticks him in bumper to bumper traffic. While sitting at a dead stand still, there are cars trying to cut in line to get further ahead. As a guy driving a blue sedan tries to squeeze in front of Joey, he moves forward to stop him. But after thinking about it, Joey decides to let the guy in. After he's in front of him, he waves and yells thank you. Joey gives the guy a lazy wave and head nod, and then something catches his eye. It's the man's license plate. It says, HEB.12:2, It's a Bible scripture. Joey has never seen this particular scripture, but he feels deep down in his heart that he needs to as soon as possible. So he pulls the scripture up on his phone, and it says, "Don't forget to show hospitality to strangers, for some who have done this have entertained angels without realizing it!" And there you have it. That explains everything. There was no Patrick Kerry. Just an angel sent by God to do one of its many jobs, which is watching over those that will accept Jesus as Lord and Savior. The Bible says, "God will never leave you in a place you ask Him to get you out of." He may not get you out as fast as you want to get out. But He will get you out in "His" timing. Everybody He created, He created with a great purpose. We don't serve a wasteful God. He loves us, His Son died for us, He wants to save us, but he'll never force us to love Him. Your freewill can be your blessing, or it can be your curse. JESUS IS ON HIS WAY!!!